THE HOUSE ALWAYS WINS

a spicy novella

THE HOUSE ALWAYS WINS

a spicy novella

ANN SCHREIBER

About the Author

Ann Schreiber is an author and lifelong book lover who lives in Minnesota with her husband and stepdaughter. She's also a proud mom to two adult children and a loving grandmother to her first grandchild.

Also by Ann Schreiber:

- *Perseverance. Reinvention.* (2024): A raw and honest memoir about starting over.
- *The Top 10 Mistakes I Made My First Year as a Copywriter* (2025): A practical guide for aspiring business writers.
- *Emily's Next Chapter* (2025): Book one in the Starting Over trilogy. A warm, emotionally rich story about love, family, and the courage to move forward.
- *Jessica's New Beginning* (2026): Book two in the Starting Over trilogy. A romantic, emotionally layered journey of rediscovery and passion.
- *Liz's Forever After* (2026): Book three in the Starting Over trilogy, centered on new love, intimacy, and the unexpected paths life can take.

For more information on what Ann is reading and writing, follow her on Instagram.

A Letter to My Readers

Thank you for picking up *The House Always Wins.* This novella came to life in a very unexpected way. After finishing *Liz's Forever After,* the final book in my *Starting Over trilogy*, I felt inspired to try something new. I wanted to write a story with sharper edges, higher heat, and a different kind of emotional tension. A spicy love story set in the heart of Deadwood felt like the perfect creative detour.

Brooke's journey through grief, desire, and rediscovery pulled me in from the moment I wrote the first line, and I'm thrilled to share her story with you.

This novella also marks a meaningful moment for me as an author. A shorter version of this story is included in the *Wild Deadwood Reads 2026 Anthology,* available in paperback as of May 15, 2026, and in ebook format as of May 20, 2026.

This standalone edition you're holding includes exclusive bonus content not available in the anthology. That means expanded scenes, more profound character moments, and all the delicious details I didn't have room for the first time around.

Whether you're reading this as part of your romance rotation, your Deadwood-themed collection, or simply because you love a little heat with your heartbreak, thank you for choosing to spend your time with Brooke and Dane.

Below are a few details to help guide your reading experience. *Here are the tropes you can expect to enjoy:*

- Spicy small-town romance
- Grumpy, broody hero with a soft center
- Grieving heroine reclaiming her life

- Instant chemistry / intense attraction
- Forced proximity (hello, penthouse suite)
- Protective hero
- Found strength and emotional rebirth
- Touch of mystery + family secrets
- HEA (because Brooke deserves one)

This novella also explores sensitive and potentially triggering topics, such as:

- Death of a fiancé (past event)
- Grief and trauma related to loss
- On-page sexual assault attempt (non-graphic but emotionally intense)
- Physical altercation between characters
- Discussions of past allegations of harassment
- High-heat sexual content
- Family conflict and manipulation

Thank you again for reading. I hope Deadwood, with all its grit and charm, stays with you long after you turn the final page and that Brooke and Dane's story brings both heat and heart to your bookshelf.

With love and gratitude,

Ann

www.foxpointepublishing.com/author-ann-schreiber

Library of Congress Cataloging-in-Publication Data
SCHREIBER, ANN, author.
TOWN, SCOTTY, designer.
THE HOUSE ALWAYS WINS / ANN SCHREIBER. – First edition.
Summary: A modern-day romance set in Deadwood, South Dakota,
where grief, desire, and long-buried secrets collide in unexpected ways.
Softcover ISBN 979-8-9938504-7-4
[1. Romance / Second Chances – Fiction. 2. Romance / Alpha Male – Fiction.
3. Romance / Small Town & Rural – Fiction.]
Library of Congress Control Number: 2 0 2 6 9 3 1 3 3 5

First printing June 2026

Prologue

The sun had felt absolutely glorious the day my life changed forever. I can remember it as if it were yesterday. Hell, I can rememberit as if it were just five minutes ago.

I was sitting on a soft plaid blanket, wearing the Lilly Pulitzer shift dress I had bought just for this trip. Mitch was sitting next to me. He kept leaning forward and grazing the exposed portion of my bare leg with his finger, his expression a bit suggestive, a bit drunk.

I had a glass of Chardonnay in my hand. In front of us sat a charcuterie tray hinting at the remnants of Brie, Camembert, Havarti, strawberries and grapes, and a small container of Spanish olives. They were the fancy ones with the pits still inside.

It was the last afternoon of our trip before flying home. Our "premoon," he had called it when he had surprised me with the plane tickets and boutique hotel reservation just a few weeks back. It was a chance to steal one more week together before the chaos of the wedding swallowed us whole. In weeks from now, I'd be Mrs. Mitchell Raines.

He'd even practiced the name out loud once, grinning as he said it. "Brooke Raines," he'd declared, as though the name had been meant for me and me alone.

Now, sitting on that blanket beneath a sprawling oak, I'd laughed and told him to stop tempting fate. "You're going to jinx it," I'd teased, tossing a grape at him.

"Please," Mitch had said, catching it easily. "Nothing could jinx us."

I could still hear his voice. That gravelly, easy tone that had made me say yes after five years of dating and one long Minnesota winter spent wondering if he'd ever get around to a proposal. He finally had, on my thirtieth birthday, right after I'd finished a night shift at the medical center in International Falls. I'd come home exhausted to find candles, lasagna, and a tiny wooden jewelry box perched between two stemmed wine glasses and plates.

He'd built the ring box himself, using leftover walnut from a recent job at the shop. He'd never been one for grand gestures, so I had been swept away with the thought he had put into the proposal, the ring, the box, and the getaway.

That afternoon, the vineyard stretched vast and endless around us, vines curling in even rows under the soft hum of bees. A few other couples picnicked nearby, but it had felt like the world had drawn a circle around the two of us. It was like we were in our own world. Mitch and I. Me and Mitch.

I plucked an olive from the bowl and moved it toward his mouth. "Open up, big boy," I chided playfully.

He grinned, leaned forward, and let me feed it to him. He leaned forward to kiss me. I could taste the saltiness of the olive that was still in his mouth. I moaned subtly as his tongue swept over my lips. Then I pulled away, laughing, and thought: This is it. This is happiness in its simplest form.

Then he'd coughed.

At first, it was small. There wasn't much to it. It wasn't anything that had me alarmed in any way. I'd been about to make a joke about the olive going down the wrong hole, but then the sound of his cough changed. His eyes grew wide, and his hands reached up to his throat. Seconds later, he began turning blue.

"Mitch?" I said, sitting up fast, wine sloshing over the blanket.

When he didn't answer, and his eyes simply grew wider, my instinct took over. I scrambled behind him, my heart hammering, wrapping my arms around his chest. I'd taught the Heimlich maneuver to other nurses, practiced it hundreds of times on training dummies. My hands were sure, and my movements were precise. I knew just what to do. Thrust in and up. Again, again.

"Mitch, come on. Come on," I'd begged. His body convulsed, once, twice. Nothing. The olive didn't seem to budge.

My mind screamed the steps, but my body had already betrayed me, muscles burning as I tried again, harder, desperate. His eyes rolled back into his head, and his arms fell to his sides.

We were no longer alone. Someone had shouted for help. Another voice said an ambulance was on the way. I barely heard them.

I'd kept trying, my arms locked around him until strangers pulled me away, my dress scooting up too high, but I didn't care. I'd fought them, screaming Mitch's name, clawing to reach him again. The world had gone blurry. The sunlight was too bright, my breath too short.

But when the paramedics arrived, I already knew. His skin had taken on a pallor. It was the color of death. And when they took his pulse and confirmed he was gone, I simply nodded my head. Someone had covered him with a blanket. The medical examiner came an hour later. His body was loaded into the back of an ambulance and taken away.

Two days later, I boarded a plane home to Minnesota.

Mitch had splurged on first-class tickets for the trip. But now, the seat beside me remained empty, still ticketed in his name. Somewhere below, in the storage hold, Mitch was enclosed in a polished oak casket. I didn't cry until we touched down.

I knew that Mitch choking on an olive wasn't my fault. But it was I who had fed him the olive that had caused his death. I had killed the love of my life. Even though I had replayed every movement in my head in slow motion, it didn't matter. Mitch was dead. And I was alone.

I spent the days after returning home with Mitch's mom and dad, planning his funeral. My parents took on the process of canceling all of the wedding plans. It was a terrible juxtaposition of things, telling people there would be no wedding, but there would be a funeral instead.

A week later, I returned to work, even though my boss advised me to take more time. But more time for what? When someone dies, there's not much more to do, is there? I felt like I was simply going through the motions. My colleagues didn't know what to say. So they chose silence, and that spoke to me more than their sympathy cards or flowers ever did.

I started skipping my lunch breaks. I took on extra shifts to stay busy. Yet it wasn't enough.

At home, alone in our queen-sized bed, the same memory always found me: the way the sunlight had hit the wineglass, scattering speckles of gold across his face. I remembered the way he'd laughed when I'd told him he'd eaten all the Brie.

I kept my engagement ring in the small jewelry box on our dresser. I couldn't bring myself to wear it, but I couldn't bear to put it away either. And his family hadn't asked for its return. Mitch's parents and sister, and my own parents and two brothers, had all tried to support me, asking what they could do. But how do you respond when the only thing you want is for them to give you your fiancé back? As the weeks went by, they all stepped back and returned to their own lives.

Mitch and I were still relatively young. Well, I was still relatively young. Mitch would never celebrate another birthday. In any case, our parents are still young, not yet retired. They had their own careers to go back to. And before I knew it, everyone was back doing what they did, except me.

Over the next two years, I moved through life like a ghost. Polite, efficient, invisible. And at one point, I realized I couldn't take it anymore. Almost two years to the date that Mitch left me forever, I walked into my boss's office, a flyer in my hand. It was for a traveling nurse position. "I want to do this," I said to Rebecca. She looked at the flyer, then at me. There was that look of pity. It was the only look I seemed to get from people these days.

But after a moment, she nodded her head. "You're one of the best we have, Brooke. Are you sure?"

"I just..." I paused, searching for the correct phrase. "I need to be somewhere else for a while."

When the email came a week later, confirming my first assignment at the medical facility located in Deadwood, SD, for three months in the emergency department, I felt something I hadn't felt in years. It wasn't joy. And it wasn't excitement. Not really. If anything, it was relief. As though the old song was calling to me, it was the chance to go somewhere where nobody knew my name.

And so, I cleared out the refrigerator and cupboards of food. I covered the furniture with white sheets. I turned off the water to prevent any leaks. And I locked up my house. Shortly after, I made the five-hour drive from International Falls to the Minneapolis airport.

As the plane taxied toward takeoff, I looked out the window at the passing skyline of the Twin Cities and thought about the one thing Mitch used to say whenever we played poker with our group of friends.

"Doesn't matter how many times you fold, babe," he'd tease, tossing chips into the pot. "Sooner or later, everyone gets dealt a good hand." And maybe Deadwood, South Dakota, was the good hand that I needed.

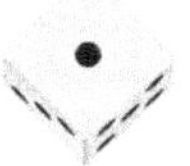

Chapter 1

It was a short flight to Rapid City, South Dakota, barely enough time for a snack and a few pages of reading, but I didn't mind. I could probably have made the drive, but my car was the one Mitch and I had bought together. Every time I sat behind the wheel, I could see the day it had been delivered to the local dealer. The memory was too sharp, too heavy. So before leaving Minnesota, I'd sold it.

The dealership in the Cities arranged for their shuttle driver to drive me to the airport and then paid me cash, which padded my pocketbook more than I'd expected. Not that I needed the money. Unbeknownst to me, Mitch had updated the life insurance policy through his job, naming me the sole beneficiary. The payout, one and a half times his annual salary, wasn't a fortune, but it had covered his funeral expenses and left enough to tuck away for a rainy day.

That rainy day fund had come in handy for the tiny rental house I'd found in Deadwood. It also meant I could pay cash for the used

SUV I'd already picked out online from a local dealer. The salesman was expecting me tomorrow to finalize the paperwork.

Though the flight was short, I had enough time to thumb through a few books I'd ordered from the bookstore back home in International Falls. I leafed through local histories of Deadwood and the Black Hills. I'd always liked learning about the places I went to, even if I was only passing through.

I read about Wild Bill Hickok and Calamity Jane, about how a gold rush had transformed a rugged gulch into a booming mining town. Then came the part that stayed with me: the 1879 fire that destroyed most of Deadwood. Over three hundred buildings burned to the ground, yet only one person had died. It was strange how quickly life could change, how one moment could erase everything you thought was permanent.

The books said the town was rebuilt, this time using brick, stone, and mortar instead of pine. That may have been what drew me there, subconsciously. It was a place that had burned down but refused to disappear.

I'd never been to South Dakota before. The idea of turning over a new leaf in a place with that kind of history felt right.

In just under two hours, the plane touched down in Rapid City. I made my way through the small airport to baggage claim, where I retrieved my single suitcase. The rest of my belongings, including boxes of household items and clothes, would be delivered to my rental house later in the week. After grabbing my suitcase off the carousel,

I found the rental car desk and signed the paperwork for a compact sedan that looked like it had seen its share of tourists.

Rapid City Regional wasn't large, not compared to MSP or the other airports I'd been through. Within forty-five minutes of landing, I was on the highway, headed toward Deadwood. Another seventy-five minutes later, I turned into the narrow gravel driveway of the small house on Williams Street that would be home for the next three months.

The key was exactly where the real estate agent said it would be, tucked beneath a ceramic planter on the back deck. The house itself was tidy and fully furnished, except for the bedroom. My new bedroom set was scheduled for delivery later in the week. Making arrangements to ship boxes, buy furniture, and shop for a car online had been oddly therapeutic. It gave me something to focus on besides the silence of my empty house back home.

Inside, the place smelled faintly of lemon cleaner and old pine floors. I spent the next couple of hours wandering from room to room, opening cupboards and drawers, unpacking what I could. By the time I hung the last few clothes in the closet, evening shadows were starting to stretch across the deck, and my stomach reminded me I hadn't eaten since morning, and the chips I had devoured on the plane.

I drove into town, following the narrow, winding roads that cut through Deadwood's historic district. It was clear why tourists loved it. The old brick buildings with ornate facades, wooden boardwalks, and saloon signs glowed against the twilight. I found a small grocery store tucked between a coffee shop and an antique store.

Despite it being peak tourist season, I still caught a few curious looks from locals as I filled my cart with staples. Eggs, milk, cheese, bread, salad fixings, a case of Diet Coke, and some lunch meats from the deli. Nothing fancy. I wasn't interested in cooking elaborate meals for one. Besides, when I was working, the hospital cafeteria would be good enough. I'd long gotten over the stigma of "hospital food."

After paying for my groceries, I loaded them into the trunk and drove back to the house. The sky was dark by the time I pulled in. I made a quick sandwich, turned on the TV for background noise, and grabbed one of the books from my bag.

As I flipped through the pages, I stopped on an old photo of Deadwood's Main Street showing men in wide-brimmed hats, women in long skirts, and the dirt road bustling with wagons and horses. The caption read: *Rebuilt after the Fire of 1879.*

Rebuilt. The word lingered in my mind.

I took another bite of my sandwich and leaned back in the chair. Maybe that was why I'd come here. Not to start over, exactly, but to rebuild. Brick by brick. Theoretically speaking, of course.

I didn't need to report to the hospital until the day after tomorrow, which meant I had tomorrow free to explore. To get my bearings. To see what kind of town Deadwood really was.

I closed the book, stacked my dishes in the sink, and realized only now that the house lacked a dishwasher. I sighed and glanced out the window. Even with the moonlight, the mountains were just faint silhouettes against the dark sky that I could only make out due to the twinkling of lights from houses on the hillsides. Somewhere out there, a new chapter was waiting for me. And for the first time in a long time, I was ready to see where it led.

Chapter 2

The sun woke me before my alarm did. It cut straight through the half-drawn blinds, a golden line across the couch where I'd spent the night. Without a bed yet, the couch had been my only option. My back protested immediately when I sat up, stiff and sore from the lumpy cushions.

I stretched, arms overhead, and muttered something unladylike before padding into the kitchen. I opened the cupboard, spotted the empty coffee maker, and realized what I'd forgotten.

"Damn it," I said aloud. I forgot to buy coffee. Of course.

Defeated, I grabbed a Diet Coke from the fridge, cracked it open, and took a long drink. The carbonation burned my throat in the best way. Caffeine was caffeine, after all.

Breakfast came next. I cracked two eggs into the frying pan. I nearly burned them, just the way I liked them. A splash of milk for fluff and a sprinkle of shredded cheese over the top. When they were done, I slid them onto a plate and sat at the kitchen table, planning out my day while I ate.

The night before, I'd jotted down a few ideas after flipping through the Deadwood history books. I'd start with a guided walking tour using an app I'd downloaded. It promised to keep me away from the heavy tourist crowds and share stories about Calamity Jane, old saloons, and even something called Deadwood's Chinatown. Who knew? Deadwood once had a Chinatown.

Next, I'd stop by the Historic Adams House, built in 1892 by pioneers Harris and Anna Franklin. I'd read that it was preserved just as they left it. Furniture, décor, even the dishes still set on the dining table, like the family might walk back in any minute.

From there, I wanted to see the Broken Boot Gold Mine and try my hand at panning for gold. For dinner, I'd already made up my mind to eat at one of the casinos in town. The Silver Spur Casino was on my list. Maybe I'd drop a few quarters into a slot machine while I was there. Do slot machines even take quarters anymore? I had no idea. I'd never been to a casino.

But before I got started on all that? I needed a shower. And actual coffee.

After freshening up, I drove into town and stopped at the same coffee shop I'd seen next to the grocery store the night before. It was

early, but the place was already busy serving locals. I found myself surrounded by construction workers in reflective vests, women in scrubs, and a few retirees reading the morning paper. I ordered a large latte and a blueberry muffin, enjoying the smell of roasted beans and warm pastry before heading out.

Following the walking tour app's directions, I parked near the spot once known as Deadwood's Chinatown. The narration in my earbuds guided me through narrow streets, pointing out historic plaques and preserved foundations. The app explained that in the late 1800s, Chinese immigrants came to work in the mines and laundries, carving out a small but prosperous community that was largely lost to fire and time.

The route wound past old saloons with names like The Gem and Number Ten, where Wild Bill Hickok had been shot in the back of the head while holding what would later be called the dead man's hand: aces and eights.

The tour ended at the Wild Bill statue, carved by Korczak Ziolkowski, the same artist who'd begun work on the Crazy Horse Memorial. Curious, I looked it up on my phone. It was over an hour away. Maybe another day, I told myself.

I walked over to the Adams Museum next and spent the next hour wandering its exhibits. I browsed the Victorian furniture, sepia photographs, gold nuggets behind glass, and artifacts from the devastating fire. Deadwood had burned, rebuilt, and burned again. And yet here it stood, restored and resilient. Once again, the thought came to mind that maybe that was what I wanted, too. To rebuild.

When my stomach growled, I decided it was time for lunch. I found a small café a few blocks away and realized, as I walked, the whole town was smaller than I'd pictured; charming and self-contained.

As I passed storefronts, I counted at least six casinos, each one tucked between souvenir shops and restaurants. I noticed a sign for The Silver Spur Casino, advertising a dinner special: *Steak and Potatoes – $18.99.* It couldn't have been more perfect because the casino was already on my list of places to hit up.

After lunch, I drove out to the Broken Boot Gold Mine, about five minutes outside of town. It wasn't far, but far enough that I didn't want to walk. The road curved around the hillside, offering glimpses of the Black Hills area through the trees.

The mine tour was short and kitschy, but I didn't mind. I panned for gold alongside a few families with kids, swirling the pan in the cool water until I spotted a few glittering flecks at the bottom. "Gold dust," the guide said cheerfully. "Worth about five cents."

I laughed, pocketed the tiny vial they gave me, and decided that was enough mining for one lifetime. It was for the kids, really. Still, I could check it off my bucket list, though it had never been on it to begin with.

From there, I drove to Spearfish for my 4 p.m. meeting at the car dealership. The process was painless. They even offered to handle returning the rental on my behalf—one less thing to juggle. I relaxed a bit as I signed the final paperwork. Ninety minutes later, I slid behind the wheel of my new-to-me Cadillac XT4, inhaling that faint leather scent that never quite goes away.

It felt good. Different, of course, but good to have something that was wholly mine again.

By the time I got back to Deadwood, the sun was dipping low behind the hills, washing the town in amber light. My stomach growled again, reminding me I hadn't eaten since lunch. The steak dinner at the Silver Spur was calling my name.

As I parked and turned off the ignition, I sat for a moment, taking in the neon glow of the casino sign. The air smelled faintly of pine and fried food.

I thought of Mitch then. How he would have teased me for spending the day on a "history binge," as he used to call it, how he'd reach for my hand in a crowd, his thumb tracing lazy circles on my skin. How we'd snuggle under a blanket on nights like this, legs tangled, his breath warm against my neck.

I missed those small, ordinary intimacies. The way a man's touch could quiet the noise in my mind. It had been so long since I'd felt that kind of closeness. Two years. Too long.

I took a deep breath and climbed out of the car, smoothing the wrinkles from my shirt. "Okay, Brooke," I whispered to myself. "New town. New start."

The lights from the Silver Spur glowed brighter as I stepped inside.

Tomorrow, I'd meet my new colleagues at the hospital. But tonight, I'd let myself enjoy a meal, a drink, and maybe a little company.

Chapter 3

I'd always wanted to visit a casino, and Minnesota had them, but they were never exactly close by. Plus, it had never been something Mitch was interested in. Sure, he liked to gamble, but his idea of gambling was a poker game with our friends around the kitchen table.

It was also a small group of friends. Most of them had moved away years ago after high school, chasing bigger and better things in cities like St. Paul, Denver, New York, and Los Angeles. One of our friends had even relocated to Paris and sent the cutest postcards every Christmas.

But Mitch and I had always been hometown people. I attended nursing school in Bemidji and returned to International Falls after graduation. Mitch entered an apprenticeship program right after high school. We hadn't been high-school sweethearts; he was two years older than I was, which struck me now because he had died at the same age I was today. That was a bit morbid, I thought to myself.

Anyway, we'd known *of* each other, but didn't really get to know each other until about seven years ago. And, as is typical of small towns, we'd been set up by family members. My older brother and Mitch's older sister had dated for a while. It hadn't worked out for them, but somehow, it had worked out for us, until it didn't. Obviously.

I tried to keep these thoughts out of my head as I walked through the sea of poker tables at the center of the casino. Mitch's poker setup at home had been a fold-out contraption he'd spread across the kitchen table. These tables, though, were the real deal. Green felt, shiny chips, and dealers in crisp shirts.

A few tables caught my attention that I didn't recognize. One had a giant spinning wheel in front, and I assumed it was a roulette table. That was about the extent of my limited gambling knowledge.

Of course, I knew how to work a slot machine. I'd played those on phone apps off and on for years, but never with real money. I walked over to one and was surprised to see that coins were no longer required. I was reaching into my purse for a twenty-dollar bill when I noticed that all the players around me had little plastic cards inserted into their machines.

I turned to the older woman next to me. "Excuse me, what's that card for?"

"Oh, that's the *Players Club* card," she said, giving me a look that made it clear I was absolutely clueless. I was. "You can get one over at Guest Services." I must have looked confused because she pointed behind me to a large sign that said exactly that.

"Thank you," I said, and made my way to the counter.

There were two people ahead of me, and then it was my turn. "I'm curious about the *Players Club* card," I told the man behind the plexiglass.

He was dressed in what I assumed was standard casino attire. Black vest, white shirt, a little too much hair gel. He handed me a pen and a small form. I filled out my information, retrieved my Minnesota driver's license, and slid it through the small window cut-out.

Five minutes later, I had my very own card. *Brooke Cassidy*, it read in bold print. Seeing my maiden name on yet another document hit me in the gut. By now, it would have been *Brooke Raines*. Yet it would never be now.

I worked my way back to the quarter slots I'd been eyeing earlier. It was a Triple 7 machine. I slipped in a twenty and pressed the button, only to realize too late that the bet cost five dollars. I won nothing.

"What?" I muttered, leaning closer to check the screen. That's when I noticed I could change the betting amount.

The woman from earlier was still at her machine. She glanced over, rolled her eyes in dramatic exasperation, and said, "Never played slots before?"

"Never even been in a casino before," I admitted.

Her expression softened. She stood and pointed to a section of machines about twenty feet away. "Those are better for beginners. Max bet is $1.25, and you've got higher odds of winning."

I thanked her and cashed out my remaining fifteen dollars. The slot machine printed a slip resembling a receipt, and then I removed my card. I next walked over to the machines she'd pointed out. I inserted my Players Club card and entered the fifteen-dollar voucher.

I pressed the *Max Bet* button and was relieved to see it cost only $1.25 this time. Nothing.

Pressed again. Nothing.

"Third time's the charm," I muttered, hitting the button one more time. Three little farmers holding pitchforks appeared in a perfect row across the center. Lights flashed. Music blared. The machine erupted in a flurry of digital confetti, and a bright "BIG WIN!" banner filled the screen.

Two hundred dollars. I'd just won $200.

Not wanting to test my luck, I cashed out immediately. At the cashier window, a young man scanned my ticket and handed me $212.50 in crisp bills and shiny coins. "Congratulations," he said with a smile.

"Thanks," I replied, tucking the money into my wallet and heading toward the restaurant.

By now, I was starving. I followed the scent of grilled meat until I reached the Silver Spur Restaurant, attached to the casino's main

floor. A man who resembled the host was speaking with another man in a black suit over a black T-shirt.

The host was good-looking, sure, but my eyes kept drifting to the man in the suit. He was everything Mitch wasn't, except for the height. Mitch had been six feet even, but this man was easily six-two, maybe six-three. Where Mitch's hair had been light blond, his was a deep, satiny black. Mitch had worn a goatee; this man was clean-shaven. Mitch had been lean and toned, but this guy filled out his suit in a way that left little doubt he spent time in the gym.

After a few seconds, he met my gaze. He didn't bother to hide the way his eyes traveled over me, my turquoise sundress, my light sweater, lingering just a bit too long on my chest. I felt self-conscious but also… aware. Mitch used to tell me I had "perfect handfuls." I blushed, both at the memory and at the way this stranger was looking at me.

He leaned in to whisper something to the host, who nodded. The man in the suit turned back to me. "Miss, are you waiting on another?"

"No, just me," I said. His eyebrows lifted, surprised.

"Very well then," he said. "Desmond, will you please seat our guest?"

Desmond, the host, nodded, grabbed a menu, and gestured for me to follow. The man in the suit went back to the computer screen, though I could still feel his gaze on me as I walked away.

Once seated, I ordered a Cosmopolitan because it sounded fancy. When it came time to order dinner, I went with the special: the steak and potatoes I'd seen advertised earlier. The waitress smiled knowingly and jotted it down.

When the food arrived, I realized I was hungrier than I'd thought. The steak looked perfect, and the baked potato steamed invitingly. As I buttered it, I noticed the older woman from the slot machines walk by with an older man who was clearly her husband, simple gold bands glinting on their left hands.

The steak was delicious. I'd ordered it medium-well, and the waitress had raised an eyebrow, as if silently judging me, but I didn't care. I wasn't interested in pink meat. Not that I'd ever tried it that way.

While I ate, I pulled my Deadwood history book from my purse and flipped to a chapter on gambling in the Old West. Apparently, by the 1870s, Deadwood had been filled with saloons and card games, some legal, some not. Gold miners had lost fortunes overnight, and shootouts weren't uncommon when luck turned sour.

I smiled at the irony. Here I was, sitting in a modern-day version of the same thing, eating steak in a room where people still tested their luck.

When I finished, I reached into my purse for cash. Two twenties. The meal had been excellent, and the place was upscale enough to warrant a decent tip. I was just scooting out of my chair when a commotion behind me made me freeze.

A familiar voice gasped, followed by frantic coughing. I turned.

The woman from the slot machine.

"Oh my God," I whispered. "This cannot be happening."

She was choking. The host was already beside her, slapping her on the back. He was doing it wrong. Completely wrong.

"Crap on a cracker," I muttered under my breath, hurrying over.

"Move," I said firmly, pushing the host aside. He stepped back, startled. My mind went instantly into clinical mode. I wrapped my arms around the woman's chest and pulled hard, up and in. Nothing. Again.

The second thrust did it. A piece of chewed steak shot out of her mouth and landed squarely on the table.

The woman sagged with relief, coughing and wiping her mouth. Her husband clutched her arm, eyes wide. Around us, people who had stood up to watch began to relax, murmuring their own relief.

"Thank you," she managed, voice raspy. I grabbed a napkin from the table and handed it to her.

"Are you okay?" I asked, even though I could already tell she was breathing fine.

"Yes, it just went down the wrong hole, is all," she said weakly, dabbing her mouth. Then she smiled. "Thank you. And I hope those $1.25 machines were good to you."

I couldn't help but laugh. "They were, thank you."

Satisfied she could sip water without trouble, I turned to leave, only to collide hard with something solid. Someone solid.

I looked up. The man in the black suit. His hands caught my shoulders before I stumbled. Up close, I could see a faint shadow of stubble along his jaw and smell the clean scent of soap, with a faintly woody undertone.

For a heartbeat, neither of us spoke. Then his mouth curved into a slow, knowing smile. And just like that, I had the distinct feeling my luck in Deadwood, or rather in life, was about to change.

Chapter 4

My heart skipped a beat at the solidity of him. Up close, literally pressed against him, he was even more handsome than I'd noticed at the host stand. And solid. His chest felt like a wall, his arms firm. Those biceps had to be bigger than my thighs, not that that was saying much. I'd always been told I had chicken legs. Curvy with chicken legs, that was me. A size four on a good day, a six around Christmas when there were too many homemade caramels and cookies to resist.

But next to this man? I felt small. Tiny. Almost delicate.

"Miss, please allow me to introduce myself," he said, stepping back only when he was sure I had my balance again. His voice was smooth, with the faintest rasp, like whiskey after dark. His gaze flicked down, and I realized with horror that the neckline of my sundress had slipped in our collision. Of course it had.

"My name is Dane Walker," he continued, meeting my eyes again. "I'm the owner of the Silver Spur Casino."

My face flushed as I adjusted the fabric back into place. "Nice to meet you," I said quickly, extending my hand.

His mouth curved into a faint smile as he took it. His handshake was firm but careful, confident without crushing. I'd always hated those overcompensating squeezes some men used to prove they were powerful. Dane clearly didn't need to prove anything. Or he was trained to know better.

"I have to thank you for what you did for our guest," he said. "She's a Deadwood native, one of our regulars."

"Oh, her?" I began. "She actually helped me earlier. She taught me how to use the slot machines. I've never been in a casino before, so ..." I stopped myself, realizing I was rambling. "Anyway, I was happy to help."

He studied me, the corner of his mouth lifting as though he found my nervous chatter amusing. "You knew exactly what you were doing. My staff is trained in the Heimlich, but clearly Desmond may need a refresher course."

"He reacted naturally," I said. "In a stressful situation, most people panic first and think later."

That surprised him. His eyes narrowed slightly, curious.

"I'm a nurse," I added, with a shrug.

Understanding dawned. "Ah. That explains it." His voice softened, the hint of admiration unmistakable. "Are you visiting? Or—" He glanced at the empty seat behind me. "Dining alone seems an odd choice for a tourist."

"I'm not visiting," I said. "I just moved here. Yesterday, actually."

His brows rose. "Moved here? To Deadwood?"

"Yes," I said, a small laugh slipping out at his disbelief. "I'm here on a short-term assignment. I'm covering for the charge nurse at the medical center. She's going on maternity leave later this week."

"Short-term," he repeated, testing the words as though he didn't like the sound of them.

"Three months," I clarified. "Maybe longer if they need me."

Something unreadable flickered in his eyes before he nodded. "Well, Deadwood is lucky to have you, even for a short while."

He turned briefly toward Desmond, who was still hovering near the woman who had choked. "If you'll excuse me," he said, "I should check on our guest. You've already done the hard part."

"Of course," I said, brushing imaginary crumbs from my dress. "It's late anyway. First day on the job tomorrow and all that."

He hesitated, eyes locking on mine again. "Good luck to you, Ms.—"

"Cassidy," I supplied. "Brooke Cassidy."

He repeated my name, slowly, as though tasting it. "Ms. Cassidy. Thank you again."

And just like that, he was gone, moving toward the other end of the restaurant to greet the EMTs who had arrived to confirm that the guest was okay. I watched as the black fabric of his suit jacket stretched across broad shoulders as he walked. I should have looked away, but I didn't.

My pulse was still hammering in my throat. Around me, the restaurant buzzed with quiet chatter again, forks clinking, glasses refilling, the clatter of everyday life resuming after chaos. But I couldn't shake the heaviness in my chest.

I'd saved a woman's life.

The thought should have made me proud. Grateful, even. Instead, it made my stomach twist. Because for all my training and experience, for all the times I'd saved strangers in emergency rooms and trauma bays, I hadn't been able to save Mitch.

He'd choked, too.

My mind flashed back. His face blue, my arms locked around him, the helpless sound that came from deep in my chest when I realized he wasn't going to breathe again. It was the same motion tonight. The same panic in the air. The same desperate rhythm of thrust and prayer. But this time, it had worked.

Why now? Why her? Why not then?

I blinked hard, forcing the tears back. The dining room suddenly felt too bright, too crowded, too alive.

I sank into the nearest empty chair, exhaling shakily. My palms still tingled, the adrenaline refusing to fade. It was strange how quickly old instincts took over. I hadn't thought. I hadn't even hesitated. My body just knew.

And then there was Dane.

The way he'd looked at me, not just with gratitude or curiosity, but with something deeper, something that made me want to both hide and step closer. It had been years since a man's touch had sent a rush of heat to my skin, but one accidental collision with him had done just that. I couldn't remember the last time I'd reacted to anyone like that.

When Mitch died, I'd buried every part of myself that wanted to be touched, wanted to be seen. Grief had left no room for anything physical. But now, here I was in a casino in South Dakota, heart racing because a stranger had smiled at me—a stranger who owned the place, no less.

I laughed softly to myself, shaking my head. "Get a grip, Brooke," I whispered.

But when I finally stood to leave, I couldn't help glancing toward the far end of the restaurant. Dane was talking with Desmond and the older couple, his posture relaxed but commanding. The woman who had choked gave him a grateful smile, and he nodded before turning his gaze straight back to me.

Our eyes met again. He smiled, small but knowing.

I smiled back, then turned and headed for the exit before I did something stupid, like linger.

Outside, the night air was crisp against my flushed skin. The lights from the casino marquee blinked overhead, reflecting off the hood of my car. I drew in a deep breath and let it out slowly.

Deadwood had been meant as a temporary stop, a place to work, to rest, to reset my life. Yet somehow, within forty-eight hours, it was already stirring something inside me I hadn't felt in years.

Hope. Attraction. Maybe even a flicker of something deliciously sensual, something I thought I'd buried with Mitch.

I got into my car and started the engine. The steering wheel felt cool beneath my palms. In the rearview mirror, I could still see the casino lights, flashing in rhythmic pulses of red and gold.

Somewhere behind those walls was Dane Walker. Handsome, confident, mysterious, Dane Walker.

I wasn't sure whether meeting him had been luck or trouble. Maybe both. But for now, I needed to put him out of my mind. I have a big day tomorrow—the first day of my future.

Chapter 5

The next morning came early.

I woke before sunrise, my stomach tied in anxious knots that only a first day in a new hospital could bring. The house was quiet, except for the refrigerator and the faint chirping of morning birds outside. After a quick shower and a breakfast bar, I slipped into a pair of navy-blue scrubs and a lightweight jacket, double-checking the hospital's address in my phone before heading out.

By seven-thirty, I was in the staff parking lot of the medical center, clutching a to-go coffee. I had taken a liking to that little coffee shop on Main Street. The hospital was modest, far smaller than what I was used to, even in International Falls, but the building looked well maintained, modern, and surprisingly busy for a weekday morning.

Inside, the air smelled of disinfectant, as most medical buildings do. I was glad, however, that I did not notice a lingering urine odor, which also seems to creep into hospitals despite the best efforts of the cleaning crews. I checked in with the front desk, who directed me toward the nurses' station where I'd be meeting Amber, the charge nurse I'd be replacing.

Amber was impossible to miss. Heavily pregnant, she moved down the hall in a determined waddle, one hand bracing her lower back while the other balanced an electronic tablet. Despite her obvious discomfort, she was cheerful and full of energy.

"Brooke!" she said as soon as she saw me. "Thank goodness you're here. I'm not sure how much longer I'll be walking upright, so I'm thrilled to have someone ready to step in."

Her smile was genuine, and I liked her immediately. She began introducing me to the rest of the team as we made our way through the ward. I said hello to the nurses, a couple of techs, and several physicians who were in and out of rooms. Everyone seemed friendly enough, though it was clear the hospital ran at a brisk pace.

"And this," Amber said, motioning to a tall man at the nurses' station, "is Dr. Ford Adams, our hospitalist. He's one of the best. Just don't let him know that."

Dr. Adams turned toward us with a smile that didn't quite reach his eyes. His white coat was immaculate, and his ID badge hung perfectly straight from the pocket. His gaze swept over me quickly, taking in my blonde hair, blue eyes, and everything in between. The heat of his stare made my skin prickle.

There was something about him. Something faintly familiar that I couldn't place. A tilt of his head, maybe, or the sharpness in his eyes. I doubted we'd ever crossed paths before, yet for a moment, I felt as though I should know him.

"Welcome to Deadwood, Ms. Cassidy," he said smoothly. "We don't get many new faces around here. Especially not ones from Minnesota, despite the proximity."

I shifted my weight, uncomfortable under his gaze. I couldn't quite place his expression, and I was pretty sure I didn't like it. "Thank you. I'm looking forward to working with the team."

"Likewise," he said, his smile tightening a fraction before turning back to the electronic chart that he had been studying.

Amber nudged me gently. "He's harmless," she whispered. "Mostly."

I wasn't so sure.

By mid-afternoon, I'd fallen into the familiar rhythm of patient care. Updating charts, checking meds, and working on discharge paperwork for a handful of patients eager to get home. My feet ached, but it was a good ache. It was the kind that reminded me I was back in my element.

I was standing at the counter, reviewing a file, when I heard a low, unmistakable voice behind me.

"Ms. Cassidy."

I turned, startled. Dane Walker stood just inside the double doors of the emergency department, looking wildly out of place among the scrubs and stethoscopes.

He wore jeans, a button-down shirt rolled to his elbows, the fabric pulled tight across his shoulders, and yes, cowboy boots. His dark hair was slightly tousled, as if he'd run his hands through it a few times. I blinked, trying to make sense of it.

"What are you doing here?" I asked before I could stop myself.

He smiled, a slow, confident curve of his lips that sent a flicker of heat up my neck. "Checking in on someone."

Before I could respond, I noticed Dr. Adams approaching from down the hall. His jaw clenched when he saw Dane.

"Hello, Dane," Ford said, his tone polite but cold. "Are you in need of medical treatment? I'm sure one of our nurses can assist you."

It wasn't what he said. It was how he said it. The air between them crackled with tension.

Dane's gaze flicked to him, then back to me. I could practically feel the standoff forming. But why? What was the history between these two?

"Dr. Adams," I said quickly, stepping forward, "I can help Mr. Walker with whatever he needs."

"You know each other?" Ford asked, frowning.

"We met at my restaurant last evening," Dane said before I could answer, his tone oddly formal. "Ms. Cassidy saved one of our guests from choking. I just came to thank her again."

Ford's frown deepened. "Ah. Of course." He glanced at me, something sour in his expression. "Well then, Ms. Cassidy, when you're done playing hero, I'll need those discharge forms prepared."

"Of course, Doctor," I said evenly.

Dane's jaw tightened, but he didn't rise to the bait. I gave him a slight nod toward the nurses' station, guiding him away before the tension could escalate.

Once we were out of earshot, I crossed my arms. "All right," I said. "How did you even get back here? You need a badge to get through those doors."

He grinned, clearly amused. "The Silver Spur contributes a fair amount to the hospital's annual fund. I suppose that comes with... certain privileges."

"I see," I said, arching an eyebrow. "So you really came all the way here just to thank me again?"

"Yes, well," he began, hesitating.

I tilted my head, waiting.

"I wanted to see you," he said simply. "To thank you in person, of course, but also to ask if you might allow me to take you to dinner tonight."

My eyebrows shot up. "Dinner? With you?"

"Unless you're otherwise engaged," he said, his tone teasing but his eyes sincere.

"I—well, I have patients to discharge. And a shift that ends at seven," I said, flustered.

"Perfect," he said without missing a beat. "I'll pick you up."

"Mr. Walker—"

"Dane," he corrected, that lopsided grin returning. "Call me Dane."

"Dane," I said, lowering my voice. "I don't usually mix work and..."

"Dinner?" he offered.

"Exactly."

"Well, you're not working *then*, are you? And, we don't work together," he said, his gaze holding mine with quiet challenge. "And besides, I'd like to get to know you better, Brooke. You said yourself. You're only in Deadwood for a short time. No reason to wait."

I exhaled, torn between common sense and curiosity. "All right," I said finally. "Dinner."

His smile widened. "I'll be at your house, half past seven."

And just like that, he turned and walked out, leaving me standing in the middle of the emergency ward with my heart pounding as if I'd just sprinted a marathon.

By the time 7:30 rolled around, I'd convinced myself at least three times that agreeing to dinner was a mistake. But curiosity, and maybe a flicker of something stronger, won out.

Dane picked me up outside the house, and as I was walking out to his car, a fancy, shiny BMW, I realized I had never given him my address. Shaking it off, I figured it was probably not difficult for a wealthy business owner in a small town to figure out which house the newcomer had rented.

Instead of taking me somewhere fancy, he drove us to a saloon-style restaurant just off Main Street. The place looked like it had been pulled straight from a western movie with wooden swinging doors, tin ceilings, antique photographs on the walls, and servers dressed in old-timey outfits.

Inside, the scent of grilled meat and whiskey hung in the air. A live band played soft country rock in the corner, and the chatter of locals filled the space.

"This is Deadwood," Dane said as he pulled out my chair. "Loud, a little ridiculous, and proud of it."

I laughed, relaxing for the first time all day. "It's perfect."

Dinner was surprisingly easy. We talked about where we'd grown up, he in Rapid City with his mother and half-brother. His father had passed away when he was young. I shared that I grew up in Walker, MN, and relocated with my family to International Falls when my father received a job opportunity on the U.S.-Canadian border. I'd lived there ever since, aside from my time away at college.

We went on to discuss our favorite small-town quirks and the kind of people who ended up in a place like this. He told me stories about the Silver Spur and the challenges of running a casino in a historic district.

At one point, though, my curiosity got the better of me. "So," I said, setting down my fork, "what's the deal between you and Dr. Adams?"

He paused, a flicker of annoyance crossing his face. "That's a story best left for another day."

I was surprised by his response, but chose to let it go.

He leaned back in his chair. "I'd rather not spoil a good meal." There was something in his tone, a warning, maybe, but it only intrigued me more.

The rest of dinner flowed easily, full of laughter, teasing, and a few lingering glances that said more than either of us dared to put into words. When the check arrived, Dane slipped his card to the server before I even had a chance to reach for my purse.

"Don't even think about it," he said when I started to protest. "You saved one of my regulars. Dinner is the least I can do."

Outside, his car gleamed under the saloon's neon sign; its polished surface reflecting the gold and red lights of Deadwood's nightlife. Once again, he opened the passenger door for me with an old-fashioned courtesy that caught me off guard.

The short drive back to my house was quiet, but not awkward. Every so often, I caught him looking at me out of the corner of his eye.

When he pulled into the narrow driveway, he turned off the ignition but didn't move right away. The soft instrumental track still playing through the car speakers seemed to thrum in the silence.

"I enjoyed your company this evening," he said finally.

"Me too," I admitted.

He smiled and got out, circling the car to open my door before I could even reach for the handle. "Let me walk you to the door," he said.

The porch light cast a soft halo around the front steps as we climbed them. The night had deepened into that kind of quiet that only small towns know, with crickets in the grass and the occasional rustle of leaves from a squirrel or other critter.

"I really do appreciate the invitation," I said, fishing my keys from my purse. "It's been a long time since I've… well, since I've had a night like this."

"I'm glad," he said, his voice low. "You deserved it."

I smiled, but as I reached the door, I instinctively pressed a hand to my lower back and stretched slightly.

He noticed immediately. "You all right?"

"Fine," I said quickly, laughing it off. "Just sore. I've been sleeping on the couch while I wait for my bed to be delivered."

He raised an eyebrow, his lips curving into something halfway between a smirk and a grin. "Ah. A good bed can make all the difference," he said, his tone warm and unmistakably suggestive.

I felt the heat rise to my cheeks. "I'll, uh, keep that in mind," I said, forcing a small laugh as I turned the key in the lock.

He stepped a little closer. Not uncomfortably so, but close enough that I could feel the warmth radiating from his body and the faint scent of his cologne.

"Well," I began, my voice catching slightly. "I should probably—"

Before I could finish, he leaned in, his body brushing lightly against mine, one hand braced on the railing behind me. The world seemed to narrow to the space between us, the pulse in my throat pounding like a drum. When he tilted his head toward mine, instinct took over. I pulled back, my shoulders pressing against the porch railing.

He froze immediately, eyes searching mine.

"I don't kiss on the first date," I said, my attempt at a smile coming out softer than I intended.

"Ah," he said, a slow grin spreading across his face. "So this was a first date?"

"I didn't say that," I countered, though the words came out breathier than I'd hoped.

He chuckled, the sound deep and low. "I think you just did."

Then, instead of leaning in again, he took my hand gently in his. His touch was warm, intentional. He turned my palm slightly, brought it to his lips, and pressed a light kiss to the back of it.

My breath hitched.

"Well then," he said softly, still holding my gaze. "We'll have to do this again."

He released my hand, stepped back, and nodded once before heading down the steps toward his car. I stayed there on the porch for a long moment, my pulse still racing, my fingers tingling where his lips had been.

When his taillights disappeared down the road, I finally let out the breath I'd been holding. Something was happening here, and it was something I wasn't sure I was ready for. Yet, as I stood in the quiet night, the echo of his kiss still ghosting over the skin of my hand, I couldn't deny it.

Chapter 6

Time seemed to be passing by in a blur. Nearly two weeks had passed since my arrival in Deadwood.

Amber was now the proud mother of a baby boy. She'd sent photos to several staff members, and the nurses had passed their phones around so everyone could see. I was happy for her, genuinely, but I couldn't help wondering if things had turned out differently, if I might have been a mother by now, too.

Work kept me busy. I was on a rotation of four twelve-hour shifts followed by three days off, then rinse and repeat. My new furniture had finally been delivered, which meant my back no longer ached from sleeping on the couch. Having a dresser and bedside tables again felt strangely comforting, like reclaiming small pieces of normalcy. My moving boxes had arrived as well, and it felt good to unpack a few familiar things: photos, books, clothes. I finally had drawers for my underwear instead of plastic bags in the closet.

The days were long but satisfying. I'd handled everything from broken bones to dehydration to a tourist who had drunk too much on Main Street and mistaken a stairwell for an elevator.

But it wasn't the patients who wore me down. It was Dr. Ford Adams.

Every time I ran into him, he left me feeling unsettled. He was a good doctor; that much was clear. Sharp, competent, and confident. But there was something behind those dark eyes of his, a kind of watchfulness that made my skin crawl. His hair was neatly styled, his smile perfectly measured. But was it really a smile, or a sneer disguised as one?

He'd stand too close sometimes, lowering his voice when he spoke to me, his tone a little too smooth. And though he was polite, there was an edge beneath it. It was something possessive, almost predatory.

One afternoon, I bent over a patient's bed to adjust an IV line, and when I straightened, I caught him staring at my ass, and then, as I turned, my breasts. Not subtly. His gaze was fixed, dark, and unapologetic. I wanted to say something, but the words froze in my throat.

Another time, I was charting alone in one of the smaller exam rooms when he appeared in the doorway, leaning casually against the frame.

"Everything all right in here?" he asked.

"Fine," I said quickly.

He lingered longer than necessary before finally walking away, and when he did, I let out a breath I hadn't realized I was holding.

I couldn't explain why, but I was glad I'd never been alone with him behind a locked door.

I hadn't seen Dane since our dinner at the saloon.

Not for lack of trying. I'd even stopped by the Silver Spur one evening for dinner, hoping to run into him. But he wasn't there. I told myself it was for the best; my focus should be on work, not a charming casino owner who made my pulse race.

Then, one night, after a particularly grueling shift, my phone lit up with a text from an unfamiliar number.

I'm sorry I've been away. Business in Rapid City. Would you do me the honor of joining me for a late dinner this evening?

My heart gave a small, traitorous flutter. I typed back, Who is this?

A moment later came the reply:

My apologies for my ignorance. This is Dane Walker. How about it? Dinner tonight? Surely you must be hungry after a long day. I've asked the chef to make some Deadwood favorites for us.

The invitation was tempting. I was tired, hungry, and, if I was honest with myself, a little lonely. I glanced at my watch, the one every nurse relied on, and realized it had been at least six hours since I'd last eaten.

In the mirror above the small bathroom sink, I barely recognized myself. My hair was slightly mussed, dark circles were forming under my eyes, and my scrub top wrinkled from the day. Still, a little mascara and a change of clothes could fix that.

That actually sounds nice, I typed back. Can I meet you at the casino in twenty minutes?

I'll be waiting.

I dug through my closet and pulled out a pair of dark skinny jeans and a red-and-white button-down blouse with flowy sleeves. At first, I buttoned it all the way up, then paused. What the hell, I thought, leaving the top two buttons open. In the mirror, I caught a glimpse of the curve of my breasts. Just enough, but not too much.

Since it wasn't quite dark yet, I decided to walk. The casino was only ten minutes away, and I'd recently found a shortcut: a small walking path that connected Williams Street to Main. The evening air was cool and pine-scented.

When I reached the entrance, Dane was waiting just outside.

He looked devastatingly handsome in faded blue jeans and a plaid button-down shirt, the sleeves rolled to his elbows. It wasn't the polished businessman I'd met that first time in his tailored suit or even that first time we had been out to dinner. This was something else. He appeared more rugged, more real. His shirt was unbuttoned just enough to reveal a smooth, hairless chest beneath.

"Brooke," he said with that easy smile. "You made it."

"I said I would," I replied, though my voice came out softer than I intended.

He gestured toward a side entrance. "I thought we'd eat somewhere a little quieter tonight."

He led me through a hallway to a private dining room just off the main restaurant. A small round table sat in the center, set for two, with a single candle flickering between us.

"Forgive me for being presumptuous," he said. "It's just that this town gets a bit lonely, seeing the same faces every day. So, I'm grateful for your company."

I blushed. What was it about this man that made me blush like a schoolgirl?

The dinner was everything he promised. His chef had prepared a mix of regional favorites, including crispy chislic, something I'd never tried before, Indian tacos, and tiny bison sliders. By the time I was done, I was full and happy, my earlier exhaustion replaced by a warm, pleasant buzz from the wine.

"This music is beautiful," I said, noticing the soft, melodic tune playing in the background.

"It's my own playlist," he said, standing and rounding the table toward me. "I get tired of the music in the main dining room. Too loud. Too predictable."

He extended his hand, his eyes catching the candlelight.

I hesitated. "What are you—"

"Dance with me, Brooke," he said quietly. "Indulge a lonely man."

I hesitated for only a second before taking his hand. His fingers wrapped around mine. They were warm, confident, unhurried. He pulled me gently to my feet and placed one hand at the small of my back. The touch sent a spark through me.

We swayed slowly to the rhythm, our bodies moving together in an easy rhythm. He asked me about the hospital, and I found myself telling him more than I'd intended.

"It's a good place," I said. "Busy, but the team's solid. Though..." I paused, my cheeks heating. "There's one doctor I could do without."

"Dr. Adams?" Dane asked, his tone casual but his eyes sharp.

I looked up, surprised. "How did you—"

He smiled faintly. "Small town."

"He's an excellent doctor," I said carefully. "But he makes me uncomfortable. I don't know why. There's just something about him..."

I felt Dane's body tense slightly, though his expression didn't change.

"I'd keep your distance," he said after a moment. "He's not one of my favorite people in Deadwood."

There it was again. That quiet warning, the one he'd hinted at before. I wanted to ask why, but something in his tone told me not to press. Instead, I changed the subject, asking about his casino and how he'd gotten into the business.

He smiled, the tension easing from his shoulders. "It was my family's. My grandfather started it when gambling was first legalized in Deadwood, and my dad eventually took it over. My mother ran it after he passed, until I came of age. I've been at the helm ever since I turned eighteen."

"It must have been a lot of responsibility at that age," I said.

He chuckled softly. "It was. But it taught me everything I know."

The song changed, and the tempo shifted to a slower, more profound tempo. Dane's arm tightened around my waist, pulling me closer. I felt his breath warm against my temple. I could feel the strength of his body pressed against mine: his strong arms and his tight abs.

Then his lips brushed the curve of my neck, lightly at first, then again, lower. My breath caught. It had been so long since a man had touched me like that. Mitch had been the only one. My first. My only.

I tilted my head back, a quiet sigh escaping as his lips traced the line of my jaw. Then, suddenly, his mouth was on mine. Hot, insistent, his tongue sliding against mine, tasting, teasing.

The kiss deepened, and before I realized it, we were moving, his body guiding mine until my back pressed against the wall. His hands roamed over my hips, up my sides, cupping the curve of my breast through the thin fabric of my blouse. His lips found the top of my chest, and I heard myself moan softly.

Oh God, what was I doing? Did I want this? Yes. Every nerve in my body screamed yes. But somewhere deep inside, another voice whispered *too soon*. I placed my hands on his chest and gently pushed. "No," I said softly. "You feel amazing, and this was... amazing. But it's too soon, right?"

He stepped back immediately, his hands raised. "Perhaps it is too soon," he said quietly. "Forgive me for getting ahead of myself."

The air between us was heavy, charged, and a little sad.

"Shall I take you home?" he asked.

I nodded. It was late anyway, and I had to be at the hospital by seven.

The drive was quiet but comfortable, for all of the five minutes it took. When we reached my house, he walked me to the door. He took my hand, pressed a soft kiss to it, and said, "Goodnight, Brooke. Until next time."

Once inside, I stripped off my clothes and slid naked beneath the covers, the cool sheets against my warm skin. My body still hummed with the memory of his touch. As I stared at the ceiling, one question circled my mind again and again. Where could this night have gone, if I had let it?

That thought leaves me wanting more, and since it is too soon to get it from Dane, I decide to take matters into my own hands. I reach over and open the drawer of my bedside table. Inside, I grab the pink vibrator from its box. I'd bought it before making the move to Deadwood, but hadn't used it yet. In fact, I'd never used a vibrator before.

Thankfully, I had already placed batteries in the device, and it was ready to go. I pushed the sheets down to my ankles and let my legs fall apart. I reached down with the vibrator, pressing the button to take it to its lowest setting. "Oh," I mumbled, surprised by the sensation with just that first push of the button.

I decided to see what this pleasure stick could do. I pressed the button repeatedly. By now, the device was in all its glory. I rubbed it over that delicate place between my legs and let it work its magic. I was about to insert it to see what more it could do, but I could already feel an orgasm building inside me.

And so I let it happen. Alone in the tiny rental house in Deadwood, SD, I gave myself an orgasm. It was delicious, yet lonely, and for a moment, I wished I hadn't pushed Dane away. Not that we were anywhere near the point of intercourse. But his kiss and his hand on my breast had felt amazing.

I got out of bed and padded down the hall to the bathroom, running a washcloth under hot water before cleaning myself and rinsing the vibrator. Then, I returned to bed. Alone.

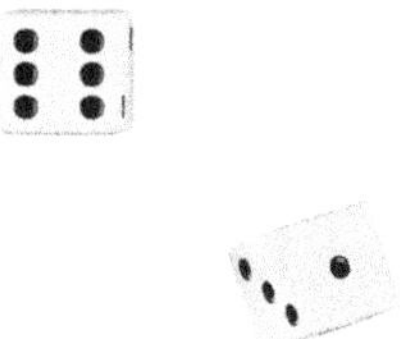

Chapter 7

When I woke the next morning, it felt as though I hadn't slept at all. I'd drifted in and out through the night, half-dreaming, half-remembering the heat of Dane's hands on my body. Each time I closed my eyes, I felt him again—his breath on my neck, the press of his lips, the strength of his body.

And each time, I jolted awake, guilt settling over me like a heavy blanket.

For so long, I had reserved every part of myself, including my touch and my heart, for Mitch. But the feel of Dane against me had been intoxicating, electric. Even though I was the one who had stopped things, it had left me aching, wanting, and confused about what that meant. And though my vibrator had given me a lovely orgasm, it simply hadn't been enough.

By the time I dragged myself out of bed and into the shower, I felt like I'd been run over. The hot water beat against my skin as I leaned my head against the cool tile, trying to rinse away both exhaustion and temptation. It didn't help much.

I worked mousse through my damp hair, twisted it into a ponytail, brushed my teeth, and dressed in a fresh pair of scrubs. My reflection in the mirror looked as tired as I felt.

Ten minutes later, I was on my way to The Daily Grind. The little coffee shop had become a morning ritual. It was one indulgence I refused to give up.

The bell chimed as I stepped inside, the warm scent of espresso and cinnamon pastries wrapping around me. I joined the line, pulling out my phone to scroll mindlessly through texts from family and friends at home when I felt someone step up behind me.

"Nurse Cassidy."

I turned, startled. "Dr. Adams! I—uh—didn't expect to see you here."

"Good morning," he said, his voice low and overly formal. "A pleasure to run into you." He smiled, though as always, it didn't quite reach his eyes.

Something was unsettling about how he looked at me. It felt like he was taking an inventory. His gaze trailed down my body before returning to my face, unbothered by being caught. I tugged lightly at the hem of my scrub top, wishing for a lab coat.

"What brings you here?" I asked, trying to sound casual.

"I could ask the same of you," he said, his tone almost teasing.

"The Daily Grind makes the best coffee in the Black Hills. I thought I'd make a pit stop before my rounds."

"Yes, they do," I replied politely, glancing toward the counter, hoping the line would move faster.

He leaned closer, just slightly. "How are you settling into Deadwood so far?"

"Oh, it's been good," I said, forcing a smile. "Between the long shifts and unpacking, I haven't had much time to explore. But I'm enjoying what I've seen so far."

"It sounds like you could use a proper tour guide," he said, his voice dropping a register. His height suddenly felt imposing, the air between us too close.

"That's very kind of you, Dr. Adams," I began carefully, "but that's not necessary."

He stepped closer still, the faint scent of aftershave clinging to him. "You don't know what you're missing."

I opened my mouth to protest, but before I could, another voice cut through the space between us. I knew his voice before I saw him.

"Ford, I believe Ms. Cassidy has already said no."

I turned to see Dane standing just behind me, his broad shoulders filling the doorway. He wore jeans, cowboy boots, and a dark Henley that fit him far too well. His tone was polite but sharp, the warning clear beneath it.

"Perhaps," Dane continued, "you should take her at her word and let her get on with her day."

The two men faced each other in silence for a moment. They were nearly the same height, and the resemblance between them was startling. Both dark-haired, broad-shouldered, commanding. But where Ford's eyes were cold and assessing, Dane's held warmth. Fire, even.

For a fleeting second, I wondered if they were related. But then I remembered their names. Walker and Adams. No connection there. Only hostility.

"Thank you, Dane," I said, breaking the tension. "I appreciate that. And Dr. Adams, I'll pass on the offer. Again."

I stepped forward as the barista called me up. "Vanilla latte, extra shot of espresso," I said quickly.

When I turned back, Ford was gone. Dane, however, remained, arms folded across his chest, watching me with an unreadable expression.

"Would you like a coffee?" I asked, gesturing toward the counter.

He gave a faint smile. "Americano, please." Before I could protest, he handed his credit card to the barista.

"Dane, that wasn't necessary," I said as we stepped toward the door, steaming cups in hand.

He shrugged. "I wanted to."

Outside, the morning sun was climbing over the hills. I glanced at my watch. Fifteen minutes until my shift. Not enough time to linger, but enough that I didn't want to rush off just yet.

"About last night," I began.

He reached for my free hand, gently guiding me to the edge of the sidewalk as a small group of hikers passed by. "No," he said softly. "Let me speak first."

I swallowed, suddenly aware of how close he was.

"I'm sorry if I was too forward," he said, his eyes searching mine. "But I don't regret it. Not the kiss. Not the way you felt in my arms. I find myself thinking about you more than I should."

The honesty in his voice stole my breath. "I… find you attractive, too," I admitted, my cheeks warming. "But what are you doing here, really? Don't you have coffee at the casino?"

He looked briefly irritated, then sighed. "I saw Ford in here with you. I don't like him, Brooke. I don't trust him." His tone left no room for doubt.

"I can handle myself," I said, though a part of me appreciated his protectiveness.

"I believe you," he said, a faint smile tugging at his mouth. "But that doesn't mean I want you anywhere near him."

Before I could respond, he lifted my hand to his lips. "Now," he murmured, brushing a kiss over my knuckles, "allow me to redeem myself. Dinner again? Or perhaps something different tomorrow? I believe you're off."

He remembered my schedule. That small detail sent a thrill through me.

"I'll think about it," I said, trying to hide my smile.

"I'll text you," he promised. And then he was gone, striding down the street toward his casino as if nothing had just happened.

By the time I reached the hospital, I had just enough time to clock in before shift change. The night nurses were bleary-eyed, passing off notes and updates while I scanned the charts on my tablet. A dozen patients, two new admits, and a stack of discharge paperwork waiting for signatures.

Once the morning chaos had settled, I began assigning nurses to rooms and making rounds. The rhythm of the hospital was its own kind of comfort. I appreciated that it was predictable, structured, and purposeful, even in an emergency department.

About an hour later, I was hunting down one of the doctors to sign discharge papers for an elderly patient who'd taken a tumble down some stairs the night before. I turned the corner and nearly walked straight into Dr. Ford Adams.

"Nurse Cassidy," he said, that smug half-smile curling his mouth. "What a pleasure to see you twice in one morning. I'm only sorry our earlier conversation was so rudely interrupted."

"I don't think Dane meant anything by it," I said carefully.

"Oh, *Brooke*, Dane Walker and I go back a long way," he said, placing a strange emphasis on my name. "He meant every word of it."

He stepped closer, lowering his voice. "But let's not dwell on that. I'd rather encourage you to revisit my offer. A private tour of Deadwood to some of the less touristy spots, maybe a local favorite or two. Tomorrow?"

I resisted the urge to roll my eyes. "That's kind of you, Dr. Adams, but I'll have to pass. I already have plans tomorrow."

He studied me for a beat, and I knew he caught the flicker of a smile I couldn't quite hide.

"With Mr. Walker, I presume?"

I said nothing, stepping to the side to move past him. But as I did, he reached out and grabbed my arm. The touch was light, but it stopped me cold. "I said," I repeated evenly, pulling my arm free, "no thank you."

He held my gaze for a moment longer, something unreadable flashing in his dark eyes. Then he nodded slowly, a thin smile crossing his face.

"Of course," he said softly. "No harm in asking."

I turned and walked away, my pulse hammering. Behind me, I could still feel his eyes on my back long after I disappeared around the corner.

Chapter 8

I was saddened not to hear from Dane by the end of my shift. And I didn't hear from him by the time I got home, or by the time I slipped beneath the sheets. I was nearly asleep the second my head hit the pillow, so I missed the text he sent shortly before midnight.

> *I am afraid that the day got away from me. However, Brooke, I would very much like to spend the day with you. If you would be so kind as to accept my invitation, I believe we can get to know each other better, and you can also explore the Black Hills and see why I love this area so much.*

It was a rather long text, and I was sad I didn't see it until I woke up the next morning a little past seven. I grabbed my reading glasses off the bedside table to make sure I'd read it correctly, then typed my response.

I am so sorry I missed your text. I was exhausted when I got home last night.

Almost immediately, three dots appeared, bouncing. The man must have had his phone in his hand.

I hope you received the rest your body needs for a fun day. Please don't hold out on me, Brooke. Please say yes.

I smiled despite my blurry eyes. I set my head back on the pillow and closed my eyes for just a moment, weighing my options. Was there any rule about how long you're supposed to wait before moving on from grief? It had been two years. And I was lonely. Plus, there was something about Dane that pulled me in, and it wasn't just his looks. Though that was definitely a bonus.

I sat up, grabbed my phone again, and looked at his message, knowing he was waiting.

I quickly typed: *Why not. Where should I meet you?*

Dane's response: *I will pick you up. Be ready in thirty.*

Thirty minutes? This early in the morning? That wasn't nearly enough time to shower, dry my hair, and put on makeup. I flew out of bed, tossing clothes behind me on the way to the bathroom. This little house didn't have an ensuite, which I sorely missed, but it was just me here. I prayed no one was peeking through the windows at my stark-naked sprint down the hall to pop a pod in the coffee maker—no time to run to the coffee shop.

As the coffee brewed, I raced through the shower, washed and conditioned my hair, then ran a razor quickly up and down my legs. Not perfect, but good enough. After showering, I wrapped my hair in a microfiber towel to absorb excess water while I brushed my teeth. Then I plugged in the dryer and got my hair as dry as possible before the doorbell rang.

He was early. I looked at my watch. Five minutes early. Clearly, he didn't understand how much a woman could tackle in five minutes.

"Be right there!" I called, grabbing my silk robe from the hook on the back of the bathroom door. There was no way I'd wriggle into jeans and a top fast enough. I cinched the robe tighter and opened the door.

Dane stood there with a bouquet of daisies. They were bright white and sunny yellow. I couldn't remember the last time Mitch had brought me flowers. He saved that for my birthday or Valentine's Day, never just because.

Dane's jaw dropped when he saw me, clearly not expecting the robe. "I was still in bed when I responded to your text," I said, tugging the robe closer. Not because I was afraid of him seeing anything, but manners. And I wasn't precocious.

"I'm sorry," he said, a hint of color touching his cheeks. "Would you like me to wait in the car?"

"Umm..." I started, unsure. Then, "No, please, have a seat in the living room. I just need five minutes."

"These are for you," he said, thrusting out the bouquet. If I didn't know better, I'd say Dane Walker was a little off his game.

"Thank you. They're beautiful and unexpected," I said. I took them into the kitchen, one hand on the flowers and my other holding the robe closed. I set the flowers on the counter and reached up to the high cabinet where I'd seen a vase while unpacking. It was just out of reach.

Dane moved up behind me as if to grab it, then stopped short. "Uh—" he started, then fell silent.

I turned, confused by the look on his face. Was that pain? "Are you—" I began, but he lifted a hand.

"I'll take care of the flowers," he said, clearing his throat. "Why don't you finish getting ready? We have a big day ahead."

Still unsure what had gotten into him, I nodded and hurried back to the bathroom. It wasn't until I caught a glimpse of myself in the mirror that I understood. The front of my robe had hitched high on my thigh, and in the back, it barely covered me at all. My bare ass had been hanging out for the world and Dane to see.

Well. That explained the throat-clearing.

I dressed quickly: a soft cream tee under a denim jacket, black-and-cream plaid shorts, and sandals. I tossed socks and tennis shoes into my backpack in case we ended up hiking. A quick swipe of mascara and tinted balm, a light brush through my hair, and I was presentable.

I found Dane in the living room, placing the daisies in the vase he'd located, water already added. He glanced up when I entered. His gaze warmed, resting on my face.

"Ready?" he asked.

"As I'll ever be," I said, grabbing my bag.

I decided not to mention the bare-all moment at the door, or whatever he'd seen in the kitchen. Instead, once we were in the car, I opened the conversation.

"So, what's the plan for the day?"

Dane cleared his throat again. He'd been doing that a lot this morning. He shifted in his seat as he pulled away from the curb, as if to reposition something. I tried to keep my mind from just what he needed to reposition, but couldn't help myself.

"I thought we'd start with breakfast. There's a great café in Hill City. The chef is our head chef's brother. The food is excellent."

My stomach rumbled. I hadn't realized how hungry I was. "Sold."

"And then?"

"Impatient, Ms. Cassidy?" His mouth tipped in amusement, the tension easing out of his shoulders.

"Just curious."

"I thought Mount Rushmore, then a quick drive by Crazy Horse. We'll end the day with a drive through Custer State Park. If we're lucky, we'll spot bison. And donkeys."

I laughed. "Donkeys?"

"They're a tourist highlight," he said, then added, deadpan, "Hopefully they'll show and not make an ass out of me."

It took a second to land. I blinked. "Did Dane Walker just make a joke?"

"Do you think I can't be funny?" He looked wounded.

"No, I just—"

"Brooke, I'm kidding," he said, chuckling. "That joke's older than half this town. People come here for work and never have time to see anything. Today, you get to play tourist. And I'll be your guide."

I felt a little like a schoolgirl, giddy at the prospect. I knew myself well enough to know that if left to my own plans, I'd spend the next three months working and maybe peeking at a few attractions, if that.

"If we have time," he added, "I want to take you on a short hike. Two miles. Think you can handle it?"

I laughed, relieved I'd packed tennis shoes. "Challenge accepted."

Breakfast in Hill City was exactly what I needed: hot coffee, fluffy pancakes covered with a thin layer of lemon curd, and eggs that tasted like they'd come from a farm down the road. Dane ordered a skillet, then insisted we split a side of their famous cinnamon roll "so that you know what you've been missing."

"I'm going to need that hike," I said, licking frosting off my thumb.

"I planned accordingly," he said, smugly, and I kicked him lightly under the table.

The drive to Mount Rushmore wound through hills thick with pine. The presidents rose into view all at once. They were unexpected and massive, pale against a razor-blue sky. We lingered at the overlooks, shoulder to shoulder, while a breeze lifted the ends of my hair. He kept up a running commentary, providing bits of history and a few stories he'd heard growing up, just enough to make me feel like I was seeing it through local eyes.

From there, we headed to the Crazy Horse Memorial. We drove up to the overlook at the park and took in the sight from the car. Dane explained that we didn't have time to do a tour today, if we wanted to enjoy Needles Highway and the Wildlife Loop Road.

"Hungry?" he asked after a few minutes of observation.

"Always."

We stopped at a roadside café for burgers and fries. I ordered a bison burger and found myself liking it more than I expected. I'd now tried two bison burgers during my time in South Dakota, and wondered if I could ever eat a regular hamburger again. "Probably not the best pre-hike meal," I said, wiping my fingers, "but delicious."

"We'll walk it off," he said, eyes lingering just a second too long on my mouth.

He turned onto Needles Highway, and I pressed a hand to the window like a kid. I'd never heard of it, but the name fit. The road curled and climbed through narrow stone tunnels, rock spires stabbing the sky like church steeples. It felt like driving through some ancient cathedral carved by wind.

We parked near a sign labeled "Cathedral Spires Trailhead." In front of us rose the spires themselves, taller and stranger up close, their fluted sides catching light and shadow.

"How's your shoe situation?" he asked.

I lifted my bag. "Prepared."

We traded sandals for sneakers and headed up the trail. The path wound through granite boulders, switchbacked across sloping pine, then opened into bright clearings where the spires crowded close like sentries. A hawk circled overhead. Somewhere below, water moved, hidden.

Dane kept pace beside me, letting me set the speed. When the trail narrowed, he dropped a half step behind, hand hovering near my elbow as we navigated loose gravel. Every so often, his palm settled at my back as I stepped over a crack in the rock. It wasn't much, just that warm point of contact, and still it stirred something low in my belly.

"You all right?" he asked when I paused to catch my breath.

"I'm good," I said, a little breathless for reasons that had nothing to do with the climb.

He smiled. "You're tougher than you look."

"I'll take that as a compliment."

"It is."

We hiked in companionable quiet for a while, our footsteps crunching in unison. When the trail crested a ridge, the view opened. Spires crowded the horizon, and the valley spilled wide below. Wind skated across my skin; I shivered.

"Here," he said, shrugging off his windbreaker. Before I could protest, he draped it over my shoulders. It held his clean, woodsy scent, and for a second, I had to close my eyes to take it all in.

"Thank you," I said, voice soft.

He tipped his head, studying me. "I like this," he said. "Being out here with you."

"Me too."

We followed a side path that tunneled through a seam in the granite and opened into a sheltered alcove the size of a small room. There was stone on three sides, the fourth framing a slice of sky and the far line of spires. The rock held the day's heat. It felt private. Quiet. A place where voices wouldn't carry.

I turned to say something, maybe a joke about his donkey line, anything to cut the thrum under my skin, but the words tangled. He stepped closer, close enough that I could see the faint sun-lines at the corners of his eyes and the dark sweep of his lashes.

"Brooke," he said, barely above a whisper.

My name in his voice did something to me. My pulse leaped. His fingers touched the edge of the jacket he'd given me, trailing lightly down my arm until they found my hand. He laced our fingers together, palm to palm, then lifted our joined hands to his chest. His heartbeat thudded steadily against my knuckles.

"I don't want to rush you," he said.

"I know," I whispered.

"And I don't want to stop wanting you," he added, honest in a way that felt like stepping off a cliff.

I swallowed, the world narrowing to the warmth of his hand and the quiet around us, the hush of pines, the wind threading through rock.

"Then don't," I said.

He exhaled with relief, or maybe hunger, and eased closer, his free hand skimming my waist, settling at the small of my back. The jacket slipped a little, and his fingers brushed bare skin. My breath hitched.

"Tell me to stop," he said, voice rough.

I didn't.

He bent his head. His mouth hovered over mine, close enough for me to feel the heat of it, the faint tease of his breath. He waited, letting me meet him halfway.

I rose onto my toes.

His lips brushed mine. They were soft at first, then firmer, deeper, the kind of kiss that unraveled time. I curled my fingers in his shirt, drawing him closer. He pressed me gently against the warm rock, our bodies aligning, the heat between us spiking. His mouth trailed to my jaw, then lower, tasting the salt at my throat. I heard my own sigh.

It was needy and unguarded, and I didn't recognize myself, didn't want to.

His hand slid up, slow and sure, palm fitting the curve of my side, then higher. My pulse thundered. The world beyond the stone room fell away until there was only his breath, his hands, the yes unfurling through me.

I tipped my head back, the sky a thin blue ribbon above the stone.

"Dane," I breathed.

He lifted his head, eyes searching mine. "Tell me what you want."

I wet my lips, heart racing, the answer right there on my tongue, but no words would form. I slipped off his windbreaker and my jacket underneath. They fell to the ground, and Dane moved closer, a questioning look in his eyes.

"Dane," I breathed again.

Clearly tired of my waiting to give him further instruction, he took matters into his own hands. And when I say matters, he took me into his own hands. As though I weighed nothing more than a feather, he placed his hands under me, hoisting me up and against one of the tall rocks. I wrapped my legs around him and let my head fall back against the flat stone.

Using the rock as leverage to keep me in position, he moved one of his hands along my body to my breast. Feeling me through my shirt, he met my gaze, and when I didn't stop him, he slid his hand down and under my shirt, thumbing my nipple through the lace of my bra.

I was glad I had the foresight to grab a cute, matching bra and panties set, rather than the sensible underwear I typically wear on workdays.

I gasped at the feeling of his hand against my skin. Carefully, he let my body drop just a bit, so that I could feel his erection against my center. Good God, what was this man doing to me? What was I letting him do to me? Whatever it was, I did not want him to stop.

"Brooke, you are absolutely divine," he breathed, finding my mouth was his. Whereas his kisses at the casino had been more gentle in nature, he was more rough this time. And it was both blissful and agonizing.

"We—" I began, not sure how to tell him we couldn't possibly continue here, with the risk of someone coming around the corner and finding us in a precarious position. But as much as I knew I did not want to be discovered, I did not want him to stop.

He hoisted me up again, higher this time, so that my breasts were now even with his mouth. "Oh God," I moaned as he shoved the material of my shirt up and out of the way, and took my nipple and the lace of my bra in his mouth. His tongue was heavenly as it circled and sucked. I wished that the material would simply disintegrate from the heat of his mouth, but it did not.

The heat between my legs was intense, and I was practically dripping with my juices. I wanted him. Here and now, and I no longer cared that anyone might see.

But as though he sensed exactly what I was thinking, he released my breast and returned my shirt to its position. He suckled on my neck for a moment before putting me down.

"Not here, Brooke," he said. "I will not defile you and make you a spectacle."

"But—" I pouted, missing the heat from his touch.

"Brooke, trust me, I *will* defile you." He said, leaning his left hand against the stone wall that remained behind me. With his right hand, he ran it down my shirt, circling my breasts once again before running his index finger down to my belly, stopping at the top of my shorts.

I bucked my hips forward, unable to stop myself. "I want you," I said.

He flattened his hand against my belly and slid it down between my shorts and skin, underneath the hem of my panties, and crooked his finger into my heat, just enough to make me cry out with pleasure. "Oh," I exclaimed as his lips took mine, silencing me. And with just a mild flick to the one spot that needed his touch most, he removed his hand. He stepped back and took my hand in his.

"Not now," he said. "Not yet."

And with that, he led me down the rest of the path and back to the car.

Chapter 9

Neither of us said anything when we got back to the car. I needed a minute, maybe an hour, to come down. He likely did, too. Those twenty minutes, however long they were, pressed against warm stone had been the hottest, most sensual experience of my life. And so we rode in silence.

After almost an hour of driving, I had come to terms that I wanted more from Dane. I opened my mouth to say something honest and reckless when we rounded a curve and nearly ran into a small drove of donkeys blocking the road.

"Oh my," I said, laughing. Dane laughed too.

"They love this stretch," he said. "Wildlife Loop Road. Some days they're friendlier than others. Today looks like a good day." He tipped his chin toward the cars ahead: Windows down, people handing out snacks like Halloween.

"Are they dangerous?"

"No." He reached back and pulled a bag from the rear floorboard.

"They'll eat almost anything, but they're partial to apples and carrots."

He handed me the bag with two oversized zipper bags: one with sliced apples and the other with baby carrots.

"Let me guess," I said. "Your chef prepped these."

Dane gave me a wounded look. "You don't think I can slice some fruit and vegetables?"

I grinned, and the car ahead rolled forward. Three donkeys shuffled toward us, velvety noses already working the air.

"What do I do?"

"Flat palm," he said. "Offer a piece. They'll do the rest."

They did. Two came to my window, lips gentle on my skin as they took apple and carrot, one by one. The third drifted to the next car when Dane kept his window closed, clearly content to let me have the moment. In minutes, both bags were empty, and our new friends moseyed along in search of the next generous stranger.

Dane eased the car through the cluster and back onto the open road. I dug out hand sanitizer and rubbed away donkey slobber, smiling like a kid.

"Now what?" I asked, settling back.

He was quiet for a beat. "What would you like from me, Brooke?"

The phrasing tripped me. "What do I want from you?"

"I'll give you what you want," he said, eyes on the road. "You just have to tell me."

My throat went dry. Wanting in the heat of a moment was one thing. Saying it out loud was another. "I want you," I finally said.

His mouth curved. "Then you'll have me. But first, we eat."

We drove back to Deadwood and stopped at the Silver Spur's casino buffet. It had been ages since I'd eaten at a buffet; I never knew where to start. I was grateful for a fast metabolism and the fact that twelve-hour shifts burn through just about anything. I built a plate consisting of a crisp salad, fried chicken, and a scoop of okra, and slid into a corner booth. Dane excused himself to "check on a few things," and was back ten minutes later. Desmond, the host, appeared with a plate already arranged for him, then returned with a tray of desserts. Perks of being the owner: everyone knows your favorites.

We ate in comfortable silence for a few minutes.

"What was your favorite part of the day?" he asked.

I looked at him, knowing the real answer and deciding to tease. "Mount Rushmore. The donkeys. And that bison we saw on the way out."

He held my gaze. "Is that all, Brooke?"

There it was, my ridiculous blush. "I enjoyed our hike," I said.

"Oh, you did?" His tone warmed, eyes narrowing with an intensity that didn't match the casual clink of plates around us.

Suddenly, I wasn't hungry. Not for food.

"I did," I said.

"What was your favorite part?" He slid his plate away and leaned in. "The spires?"

"They were lovely."

"Or when I lifted you and set you against the rock?"

A shiver ran through me. "That was... good. The rock was smooth."

"Yes," he said, voice lower. "Very smooth. Was that all you liked?"

"No." My voice had gone breathy.

"Was it when I took your breast in my mouth?" His eyes had gone darker, hunger threaded through them.

Heat flooded my face. Not embarrassment, exactly. More like memory, rushing back in color.

"Or when I slid my finger inside you?" he asked, voice barely above a whisper.

I nearly choked on a sip of wine.

"Would you like more of that, Ms. Cassidy?"

I nodded.

He stood and held out his hand. "Come with me."

He led me through a quiet back corridor to a brushed-steel elevator. The casino wasn't tall, just four stories, and I remembered his note about Deadwood's National Historic Landmark District and the restrictions it carried: preserve the historic character; no showy high-rises.

We stepped inside. Alone. He swiped a keycard and pressed 4.

The doors slid shut. The car hummed, and before we moved an inch, he bracketed me gently against the wall, his mouth close enough for me to feel his breath.

"Say stop," he murmured, "and I will."

I didn't say it.

The elevator ascended, a soft bell chimed, and the doors opened onto a private hall. He guided me out with a hand at the small of my back to a dark wood door. Another quiet swipe, a click, and we stepped into a gorgeous, finely decorated, penthouse apartment. For a moment, I felt like I was Anastasia in *Fifty Shades of Grey*. Maybe I was, and I didn't care. I would gladly take Dane Walker as my own personal Christian Grey—all of him.

He closed the door softly behind us. He flipped the lock and turned to me.

Within seconds, I was in his arms, pressed up against the wall, again. There was something about this man backing me into corners and walls, and I didn't give a damn shit about it. At this point, I would let him back me into anything he wanted.

Once again, he lifted me up against the wall, and I wrapped my legs around him. Leveraging the wall and his leg to keep me in place, he reached down and lifted the bottom of my shirt. I raised my arms, and he lifted the shirt up and over my head. The cool air from the air conditioning made my nipples harden at the exposure.

"Brooke, you are so beautiful," he murmured, taking my mouth in his. His tongue roamed and explored, and I gave him back as much as he took. His kisses were exquisite, but my body ached for more. It had been so long, and I had never been touched by a man like this. And never by a man like Dane.

My head fell to the side as his tongue ravaged me, moving from my mouth to my neck, and then to my breasts. I delighted in the sensation and could barely control my lust when he suddenly put me down. He dropped to his knees in front of me, placing his lips on my belly as his hands moved to the button on my shorts. He removed the button from its hole, slid the zipper down in one smooth motion, and then slid my shorts off with his hands. I started to crouch down to him with the intention of pushing him back onto the floor so that I could climb on top to ride him, but he had something else in mind.

He lifted me again, this time, my body was only covered by the silk bra and panties. He lifted me higher, my back pressed against the wall, and I was afraid I would lose balance, but he set my legs on either side of his head, his face coming into contact with my pussy. His tongue lashed out, flicking at that one spot that I had needed him to touch earlier. Within seconds, I was dripping in ecstasy, moaning his name.

My hands were in his hair, gripping with all of my might as I tried to hold myself together and pull him closer. I pulsed my body into him so that his tongue would reach just where I needed. And just as I was afraid I was about to come undone, he slowly brought me back down to the floor and over to the couch in the living room.

I stood in front of him, taking my hands and lifting his shirt over his head. What I saw underneath took my breath away. When they talk about six packs, this is what they're talking about. Dane was chiseled in the very best of ways. His biceps and pecs were both massive, and the look of him threatened to steal my composure.

"Take it off," he barked at me, his voice hoarse. Following his gaze, I realized he was talking about my bra. I reached behind my back to loosen the clasp and let my breasts fall free. His gaze darkened, almost like a vampire about to attack its prey, and he removed his shorts and boxer briefs. What I saw next stole my breath, and I found myself fighting for air.

"What do you want from me, Brooke?" he asked, repeating the question from earlier. This time, however, I knew how to answer.

"Take me, Dane," I breathed. "I am yours."

And take me he did. He pressed me back onto the couch, and I lifted my hips so that he could remove my panties. Then, he lowered his mouth to my pussy, and when his mouth took me in, I grasped the pillows on either side of me, struggling to gain purchase. I tried not to compare his obvious sexual prowess and experience with my lack thereof. He seemed to know just what to do with his tongue.

I splayed my fingers through his thick black hair again and pulled his face closer, positioning him just where I needed. And that was all it took. His tongue knew just what to do, ravishing me with every lick, with every suckle. With his mouth and tongue stroking my clitoris, I came apart. But that didn't stop him. No, instead of allowing me to recover, he kept ravaging me, and the orgasm nearly broke me.

When I started to come down, he stood up, his erection staring me in the face. For a second, I thought he wanted me to take him in my mouth, and I hesitated. Sure, I'd done that with Mitch before, but I had never made him come that way. I'd simply written it off as not being my most remarkable talent.

But that didn't seem to be what Dane wanted. He scooped me up off the couch with his arms and flipped me over his shoulder, leaving my ass exposed to the ceiling.

"Where are we going?" I asked as he slapped my ass with his bare hand. It stung, but I found it oddly thrilling.

"I told you, Brooke," he said, gently nudging open the door to a room that appeared to be his bedroom. Though it was hard to focus after the orgasm he had just given me, and the blood rushing to my head. "I will defile you."

He set me on the bed, and I reached up to put my arms around him to pull him close, but he had something else in mind. He flipped me over onto my belly and scooted my body up closer to the pillows. He spread my legs, and once again, I felt his tongue on my core. He ran it up and down, almost as though he was soothing me after the experience on the couch. But then, I felt a different sensation.

Was he? Yes, he was. I squealed and wiggled at the strange sensation as his finger entered me, slowly, in a place where no one had dared before. Mitch and I had discussed anal sex, but had just never tried it. I was surprised to find that it didn't hurt, and that I enjoyed the sensation of his finger moving slowly, in and out. Within seconds, I could feel another orgasm starting to build. As I got close to climaxing, he removed his finger and took his other hand and slid it into my wet, waiting pussy. I came on his hand, hard. "Dane, what are you doing to me?" I asked, moaning in ecstasy.

I was feeling very satisfied, but wanted more. At this point, the man had given me two orgasms. One with his mouth and another with his hand. But what I really wanted. What I needed, he had withheld.

"What do you want from me, Brooke?" he asked, this being the third time he had phrased that question. I wondered what he wanted me to tell him.

I turned and flipped onto my back, my hair splayed across the pillow beneath me, and looked up at him. He knelt over me, one hand wrapped around himself, his weight and thickness unmistakable even in the low light. It was impossible not to notice, impossible not to feel a flicker of nerves mixed with want.

I let my gaze move from him to the space between us and back again, but I didn't say anything. I didn't yet have the language for what I wanted. I'd never been in a position like this before. I never felt bold enough to ask or confident enough to make a demand.

"Brooke, I will give you anything you want," he said. "I just need you to say it."

But still, the words would not come out. Instead, I whimpered a little, and his eyes softened. "Do you want this?" he asked as I looked down at his cock.

I nodded and reached out to him. He removed his hand from his shaft and let me wrap my fingers around him. He groaned at my touch. "Brooke—" he said, but I pulled him down to me. I lifted my hips in offering. Realizing I couldn't say the words, but understanding my needs and my demand, he obliged.

I opened up to him, and he entered slowly. He entered inch by inch, and my body slowly gave way, allowing him to sink all the way in. I wrapped my legs around him, pulling him closer. He felt divine, and I couldn't get enough. He rocked into me, and I could feel his body tense as the intensity of his movements increased.

Moments later, my arms holding him tight and his mouth on my neck, he came hard, and I matched his orgasm. Three orgasms, all from this man, all in the span of an hour. He rolled off of me and onto his back, pulling me with him so that I was tucked into his side. I felt his juices dripping out of my body and onto the sheets, but I didn't care.

I had never been so sexually satisfied as I was in that moment. And part of me wondered if that was all this was. Had I just been another sexual encounter for him? Would he ask me to leave? Would he drive me home, and I would never see or hear from him again?

As though he could sense my thoughts, he whispered into my ear, "Stay the night, Brooke. Stay with me." I nodded, and we fell asleep, just like that, with his arms around me. I felt safe. I felt satisfied. I realized there was nowhere else I wanted to be.

Later that night, I shifted in Dane's bed and realized that somehow, without ever letting go, Dane had pulled the covers up and over us. The air in the room was warm and faintly scented with cedar and soap.

I tilted my head back to look at him in the dark, the faint orange glow from the streetlights tracing the lines of his face. His breathing was deep and even, a quiet rhythm against my shoulder.

For the first time in a long while, my body felt both spent and weightless. My heart, though, was another story. It thudded softly, calm yet uncertain.

I wanted to memorize this moment. The hush of the room, the heat of his skin, the ache that felt equal parts longing and relief. But beneath it all lingered a quiet question: what happens when morning comes?

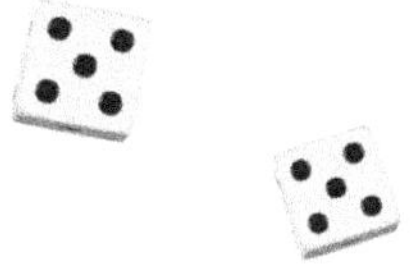

Chapter 10

When I awoke the next morning, my first thought was not to expect anything more. Part of me had even worried he wouldn't be there. He wasn't in the bed, anyway. But, when I opened my eyes, I saw him sitting in the chair beside the bed, in a dark suit, watching me with a softness that startled me.

"I didn't want to leave you," he said.

Sitting up, I pulled the sheet closer and squinted at the light edging around the curtains. "How long have you been there?"

"It doesn't matter," he said, and then raked a hand through his hair. "But I need to go downstairs to meet security. We've got a tour group coming later this morning."

"Do you want me to leave?" I slid toward the edge of the bed, then stopped when I realized I was still naked and tugged the sheet back to my chest.

"No. Brooke—no." He crossed the space in two steps and knelt in front of me. Before I could protest, his fingers found the edge of the sheet I was clutching and gently tugged it away, exposing my chest to the cool air and his sultry gaze. "I don't want you to leave, now or ever," he said softly. "But I have to work. They're a good group, and they bring real money into the casino and the town."

The only words that stuck were *I don't want you to leave*. Everything after that was a blur.

"I'll be gone awhile," he said quietly. "I don't expect you to wait. But I'd like to see you tonight. Or tomorrow."

He leaned down then, his mouth brushing my skin as he pressed a lingering kiss to one nipple, then the other, unhurried, reverent, before lifting his head and sealing the promise with a slow kiss to my lips.

"You want to have sex with me again," I said before I could stop myself. It came out flat and suspicious, as if I'd tripped over a wire in my own head.

He flinched. "Brooke, no. Yes. I would love to make love to you again." The phrasing hit something inside me and set it glowing. "But if you think that's all I want, I've said this wrong. That was never my intention."

"What is your intention?" I asked, picking up the sheet to cover myself once again.

He stood, and the suit didn't hide the muscle under it. "To keep knowing you," he said. "I'm drawn to you. Not just your beauty, though God, you are." He reached for the sheet, and I let him pull it away again. His gaze traced my skin as if he were memorizing it. "I hope you know that."

I climbed out of the bed, and I stood, bare in the morning light, and faced him. "If you want to see me, then yes. But I should go home. Text me later. We'll figure it out."

I stepped toward the bathroom, but he followed, catching my arm with a gentleness that tugged at me. He wrapped his arms around me, mouth near my hair. "Dinner tonight," he murmured.

We did have dinner that night. And the next. Over the following week, we found a rhythm without meaning to. Some nights we stayed in Deadwood, other nights he drove to various places that Dane loved. Once, he said he had to go home to Rapid City and asked if I wanted to see the house. It wasn't sprawling or flashy, not for a man who owned a casino. But the Black Hills framed it like a painting, and the quiet there felt deep and good. He explained that the penthouse was a seasonal perch. It was close enough to sleep a few nights a week during the rush, but it was never meant to be a forever home.

I told him about Mitch, not all at once. I didn't have it in me to hand over the whole story like a file folder laid wide on a desk. It came out in pieces over wine on his porch, the afternoon sun sliding along the fence, our feet up on the railing. The vineyard. The olive. How I'd tried. How the world kept turning anyway. I said it without tears, but he touched my hand like he could feel the ache threaded through my voice.

That night, he made love to me as if he understood. No pressure, no performance. Just warmth and patience and a care that settled something I hadn't known could settle. It felt like grief and comfort had locked hands and agreed to share the space for a while.

He offered his past in fragments, like puzzle pieces without edges. His father. Cancer, gone too soon. His mother had been tired, exacting, and made of iron. And a half-brother who never stayed out of trouble for long.

The brother was older, and their mother had always seemed to wrap him in a layer of protection that Dane never quite understood. Whenever his brother got himself into trouble, and it happened more than once, she handled it quietly, firmly, and without explanation. Checks were written. Meetings were held behind closed doors. Questions were waved off with a tired "It's nothing you need to worry about, sweetheart."

As Dane told it, he'd learned early not to push. His mother had carried enough weight on her shoulders without him adding to it. All he really knew was that his brother had a habit of landing himself in "hot water," as she put it, and she made sure it disappeared before the steam could rise.

And then there was the other part, the only part she'd ever shared with him outright. A portion of the casino's profits, every year without fail, was to be directed into a hospital fund. No explanation. No context. Just a firmly held promise she expected him to honor.

"Where is he now?" I asked.

"Around," he said, and that one word carried a weight I didn't poke at. We let that response linger, not needing to fill the silence with anything else.

Chapter 11

Now, I was entering my fourth week since arriving in Deadwood. At this point, the hospital felt familiar, including the squeak of the supply room door, the hum of the monitoring stations at the nurses' bay, and the way the elevator always paused too long on the second floor. Amber stopped by that morning with her baby boy, Wyatt Paul, bundled in a blue blanket. She kept him in the main lobby to spare him the parade of germs that greeted us in the emergency department. We took turns sneaking out to say hello. He was tiny and perfect, with a little knit hat and a yawn that made everyone soften around the eyes.

"Sleep?" I asked her, and we both laughed at the unfairness of the question.

"Some," she said, and her smile said it was worth it.

I floated up to med-surg to help discharge a gentleman who wanted to argue with the monitor that said he needed his meds. I found myself back in the ER by evening, triaging two sprains and a kid with a fishhook stuck in his thumb. My life was a braid of work and sleep, with an unexpected thread of Dane braided through both. It startled me how natural it felt to text him *off at seven* and have a plan waiting before I'd peeled off my surgical gloves.

We never spoke about labels. We didn't need to. He showed up, and so did I. We learned the small things: he took his coffee black; I ordered lattes with an extra shot and a sprinkle of cinnamon. He hated green bell peppers. I would never understand people who put raisins in coleslaw. He liked classic rock in the car; I could sing along to nineties ballads without looking up the words. He drove with one hand and drummed the other on the steering wheel. I curled my feet under me in every chair like I was afraid someone would take the seat if I didn't claim it fully.

We learned the bigger things, too. He kept promises. He also kept his distance from Ford Adams, and when Ford appeared in a hallway or at The Daily Grind, Dane's shoulders sharpened. I noticed it. I tucked it away. The story would come out when it needed to.

On my one day off that week, he drove us to his Rapid City place again. We walked the property line and watched a deer step out from the brush, unbothered by our presence. We ate sandwiches on the back steps and argued amiably about the right amount of mustard. When a breeze rolled down from the hills, he reached back without looking and found my hand.

We lingered there longer than necessary, the empty plates forgotten at our feet. His thumb traced slow circles against my knuckles, absentminded at first, then deliberate. The quiet stretched, charged in a way that had nothing to do with silence. When he finally turned toward me, his gaze dropped to my mouth, then lifted again, dark with intent.

He pushed the plates away and grabbed an outdoor pillow from one of the porch chairs, placing it behind my back. I looked at him questioningly, unsure of his intentions. He knelt on the sidewalk in front of the steps and took my hips in his hands, lifting them off the ground. He leaned forward and placed a kiss on my stomach before making his way down to my pussy. "Take them off," he groaned to me, and I quickly unbuttoned my shorts and pushed them and my panties down to my feet before kicking them away.

"Dessert," he moaned before placing his head between my legs and sucking my clit into his mouth. He wasn't forceful, but he wasn't gentle either. His head bobbed as he worked the magic of his tongue, licking the folds of my labia before pushing his fingers inside me as he returned to my clit. I bucked under the intensity of the moment before grabbing his head and pulling him closer, right to where I needed him to be. And he did not disappoint. I cried out in ecstasy as my orgasm took hold. Right there on the back steps with the Black Hills in view.

When I finally caught my breath again, I laughed softly, the sound half disbelief, half contentment. Dane lifted his head and smiled at me in that quiet, satisfied way that made my knees feel weak all over again.

I straightened my clothes, tugging my shorts back on and into place as he watched me with open appreciation, not rushed, not hiding what was still simmering between us. He reached out, brushing his thumb along my hip as if committing the moment to memory.

We gathered the empty plates, stacking them in easy silence. Inside, he rinsed them quickly at the sink while I walked around to close the blinds, the house settling back into darkness around us. When everything was locked and the lights off, he slipped his hand into mine again, and we walked to the car.

The drive back to Deadwood was quiet but charged, the kind of silence filled with shared glances and unspoken promises. The Black Hills faded behind us, but the heat of that afternoon stayed with me, humming low and persistent all the way home.

That night, back in Deadwood, as we made love, he moved like a man who knew my map. My body answered before my head had anything to say about it. After, we lay there with the window cracked to the night, the scent of pine and dust and summer seeping in. It wasn't the same as the first time or the second; it had lost the edge of wonder and gained something else. I hadn't known that I could feel even better.

By the end of the week, I was counting hours not to finish work, but to see Dane. And then, standing at the nurses' station with my tablet, I realized what the calendar was saying out loud: Another week down. Over one-third of my assignment is already gone.

I finished documenting vitals, signed off on a discharge, and leaned my elbows on the counter. Across the hall, one of the techs coaxed a toddler into a hospital gown shaped like a pirate shirt. The kid scowled, then grinned. The overhead lights hummed, and a monitor beeped. The world was ordinary and relentless.

Three months had sounded long when I applied. It didn't feel long now.

When my shift ended, I stepped into the evening and waited a beat before walking to the car, letting the air cool my cheeks. My phone buzzed. It was Dane.

Off soon? Dinner at seven?

I smiled at the screen, thumb hovering over the keyboard.

Off now. Seven works.

As I climbed behind the wheel, I let myself admit the simple truth: I wanted more time. More dinners that stretched late. More drives through the hills. More quiet mornings that didn't need apologies or explanations. And I had to admit, I wanted more great sex.

I put the car in gear and pulled out, the hospital shrinking in the rearview. When I first arrived, Deadwood had been a place to hide in plain sight. Tonight, it felt like a place I didn't want to leave as long as Dane was a part of it.

Chapter 12

It was near the end of another long day when I found myself crouched on the floor of the medical supply room, clipboard in hand, double-checking the end-of-month inventory. One of the orderlies had already done it, but I'd always believed in making a second review. The last thing any hospital needed was to run out of gauze or IV tubing in the middle of a crisis.

The room was narrow, the kind of place that smelled faintly of antiseptic and latex gloves. I was halfway through counting packaged gowns when I heard the door open behind me. I didn't look up. People were in and out all the time, but when the door didn't close again, I paused.

A minute passed. Two. Maybe I'd imagined it.

Satisfied that the numbers matched, I stood, brushing off my scrubs, ready to move to the next shelf. As I rounded the corner, I nearly collided with someone standing in the aisle.

"Dr. Adams," I said, startled. "You scared me."

"Well, hello, Nurse Cassidy." His tone carried a lazy amusement that didn't fit the sterile air of the supply room.

"I didn't realize you were back. I heard you'd been on holiday," I said, forcing a polite smile. "Can I help you find something?"

"Oh, I think I've found what I was looking for." He didn't move.

"Good," I said, trying to step around him. But he shifted to block my path. "Excuse me, Dr. Adams," I said, keeping my voice even.

He reached out and laid a hand on my arm, turning it so that the back of his fingers brushed slowly down from my shoulder to my elbow. My stomach tightened. I stepped back instinctively, straight into the metal shelving unit.

"Dr. Adams, please," I said. "I need to finish the inventory and enter it before shift change. Don't want to run out of supplies and all that." My voice cracked on the attempt at humor.

He lifted his other hand, catching both of my arms now, not hard, but enough to make it clear I wasn't free to leave.

"You still owe me that tour," he murmured. "I'm an excellent guide."

"Dr. Adams," I said louder, hoping the sound might reach the hallway. "I already told you I'd have to pass."

"And why is that, Ms. Cassidy?" His lips twisted into something that looked like a sneer. "You think I wouldn't make good company? I could show you the real Deadwood. The places the tourists never find. Calamity Jane's old haunts, for one. You'd appreciate that, wouldn't you? Nurse to nurse."

I forced a tight smile. "I've read plenty about her, thank you. I don't need a personal tour."

He leaned closer, and the air between us grew thin. "Is that all you're focused on, your work?" he hissed. His fingers dug into my arms. "Because I hear you've been... otherwise preoccupied."

My pulse kicked up. "Excuse me?"

He smiled without humor. "Dane Walker," he said, voice low and venomous. "He's not someone you want to associate with."

I froze. How did he know? And why would he say that? "My personal life is none of your concern," I said, my tone sharp now.

"Oh, but it is," he said, stepping forward until the edge of the shelving pressed against my back. His breath hit my face, hot and sour. "I make it my business to know who newcomers get tangled up with. Dane Walker's one of the ones you should stay far away from."

"And why is that?" I asked, my voice calm despite the fear crawling up my throat.

"He's a womanizer," Ford said flatly. "Likes the fresh ones. Plays the gentleman until he gets what he wants." His mouth curved upward, but it wasn't a smile. "You know all about that, don't you?"

"I don't know what you're talking about," I said, pushing at his chest. It didn't budge him.

He dropped one hand from my arm and lifted it to trace the line of my hair, then down the side of my neck. When his knuckles brushed the top of my breast, I jerked back, but there was nowhere to go.

"He's had his way with you, hasn't he?" Ford seethed, spittle flecking my cheek. "I can see it in your face. He's fucked you."

"Dr. Adams!" I snapped, my voice breaking. "This is completely inappropriate. I'm asking you to step back."

"Not until you give me what I want." His voice was a rasp now, and when he dipped his head toward my neck, I acted on instinct.

I slammed my heel down on his foot. Hard. At the same time, I snapped my head forward, the crown of it colliding squarely with his nose. The sound was a dull crack followed by a sharp curse.

Blood spattered across the front of his white coat. He stumbled backward, clutching his face.

I didn't wait. I darted for the door, yanked it open, and nearly collided with a solid chest.

"Brooke?" Dane's voice was rough, his hands immediately on my arms. "What's wrong?"

"Dr. Adams—he—"

Dane's expression shifted in an instant. Whatever warmth had been there drained away, replaced by something I hadn't seen before. His jaw locked, his eyes darkened. He moved me gently aside and stepped through the doorway.

"Fo-ord!" The name came out like a growl.

Ford barely had time to lift his head before Dane grabbed him by the collar and slammed him against the wall. The shelves rattled from the force.

"Dane, stop!" I said, stepping in after him, but it was too late. Dane's fist connected once, clean and hard, sending Ford's head snapping to the side.

"Dane!" I repeated, pulling at his arm. "You'll get yourself arrested!"

Ford slumped slightly, one hand pressed to his bleeding nose. "Mother would be disappointed in you, little brother," he spat.

The words hit like a gunshot. I froze, looking from one man to the other. The same jawline, the same dark eyes, the same coiled rage. *Little brother.* And in that moment, the pieces clicked together. Ford Adams was Dane Walker's older half-brother.

Chapter 13

The next few hours passed in a blur. Security had been called. Then the police. Questions came fast, one after another, until they all blurred together in my head.

Was I hurt? Did I want to press charges? Did I need a nurse?

Sexual harassment or assault was the choice I was given. And not knowing the correct answer, or maybe too afraid to pick the wrong one, I said no.

What kind of mess had I gotten myself into?

All I'd wanted when I came to Deadwood was a clean slate; a chance to outrun Mitch's ghost, figuratively, at least. But now, the very man I was growing to love, dare I even think that word, turned out to be the younger half-brother of the man who had just tried to force himself on me in the hospital supply closet.

Confused didn't begin to cover it. I was shaken, ashamed, and more than a little lost.

Both Dane and Ford had been taken into custody. The hospital administrator had also been called in. Even though I had declined to press charges, it seemed this new administrator wasn't among those whom Walker's money could buy.

And suddenly, all the little things I'd noticed started falling into place. Dane mentioning that The Silver Spur contributed generously to the hospital's annual fund. The way Amber had offhandedly said on my first day that Dr. Adams was "harmless, mostly."

And what Dane had told me about his brother: older, reckless, quick to find the line and cross it. Fights. Debts. Accusations. It all fits now. But what didn't fit was why Dane hadn't told me. Why hadn't he just said that Ford Adams, the man who'd assaulted me, was his brother? What else hadn't he told me?

And as the thought sank in, I couldn't help but think about the irony of it all. The Silver Spur had donated thousands to this hospital over the years, patching up its cracks, funding new equipment, new walls, a better image. But in Deadwood, as in the casinos, the house always wins. And in this case, "the house" looked a lot like the Walkers. Had Dane simply been paying off the hospital to cover up Ford's transgressions? I didn't want to believe that was possible, but I began to wonder.

A knock at the door startled me.

"Nurse Cassidy," a man said, stepping into the room. I recognized him from orientation: Paul Jackson, head of Human Resources. "While I understand that you've chosen not to press charges against

Mr. Adams, I'll need you to provide a written statement for our records. The legal department will require it."

His choice of words caught me—Mr Adams, not Dr.

"Yes, of course," I said quietly, staring at the wall, keeping the corner of my eye on him. Now, I wondered just who I could trust.

He nodded once and gestured for me to follow. "Sooner would be best."

I rose and followed him down the corridor, into the elevator, and up to the administrative floor. I'd never been here for anything but first-day paperwork. Sitting in HR made me feel like I'd done something wrong, even though, logically, I knew I hadn't.

Jackson's office smelled faintly of stale coffee. A brass nameplate sat on the corner of his desk. He motioned to a chair, then handed me a clipboard thick with papers. It felt outdated, this paper process, in a hospital that prided itself on being digital.

The questions were blunt:

Where did the altercation take place?

Did you report it to the police?

What is the current state of your employment?

Your mental health?

Did you seek medical attention?

And then, the one I dreaded most:

Please provide a detailed account of the altercation.

My hand shook as I began to write. I described the supply closet. It was more like a room. The way Ford had blocked my exit. The sound of his voice and the smell of his breath when he leaned in. The way his hand had brushed over my breast before I'd fought back. My head throbbed just remembering the impact from when I'd rammed him in the nose.

For a moment, I froze. Was it harassment? Assault? I wasn't even sure anymore. I unlocked my phone and typed a quick search, reading the answer right there, in black and white. Sexual assault refers to any physical sexual act that occurs without someone's consent, while sexual harassment refers to non-physical sexual conduct such as gestures or comments. By that definition, I was a victim of sexual assault.

The realization hit hard. Tears blurred the words on the page, and I pressed my fingertips to the slight bump forming on my forehead. There'd be a bruise later, a mark to remind me that this wasn't some fever dream.

"Nurse Cassidy?" Mr. Jackson's voice was gentle but tentative. He stood, then hesitated, uncertain whether to come closer. Maybe this was what it felt like to be that woman, the one others didn't know how to approach, unsure whether comfort might hurt more than silence.

"Can I call someone for you?" he asked.

I swallowed hard. "No. There's no one."

My family was hours away. My friends were scattered. The only person I'd truly connected with in this town was Dane.

As though the thought had conjured him, the office door burst open. Dane stood in the doorway, his expression torn between fury and guilt. A fresh bruise darkened his left eye socket; a cut split his lip. His suit was rumpled, and his knuckles were scraped raw.

"Brooke," he said, stepping toward me.

I held up my hand before he could get any closer. He froze.

He was the only person I knew here, the one I'd trusted—the one who could have prevented all this, if only he'd been honest.

I turned to Mr. Jackson, my voice steady despite the tremor in my chest. "Could you please ask Mr. Walker to leave?"

Chapter 14

Two weeks had passed, and I'd spent every minute of them wondering how everything had gone so wrong so fast.

The hospital had placed me on paid administrative leave while the administrators and legal team determined "next steps." Their wording. It sounded so formal. So detached.

When the call came that morning, it was short and to the point: *The investigation has concluded. You are cleared of any wrongdoing.*

No wrongdoing on my part. The words felt clinical, like they belonged in someone else's story. But I was relieved nonetheless.

I'd kept myself busy, or at least tried to. I cleaned. I reorganized the kitchen twice. I caught up on laundry I didn't even realize I had. I'd even painted my fingernails and toenails—a deep red. But mostly, I sat with my own thoughts.

And Dane hadn't called. He hadn't texted. He hadn't even sent one of his formal, polite messages like before.

I'd asked Mr. Jackson to have him leave that day, and I knew that probably stung. But if he genuinely cared, wouldn't he have tried? Wouldn't he have at least knocked? He knew where I lived. And I hadn't blocked his number. The silence was its own kind of answer.

I'd only left the house a handful of times in the past two weeks, primarily for groceries or air. I'd avoided my usual haunts: no coffee at the local coffee shop, no local market. Instead, I drove into Lead, where nobody knew my name. I stocked up on food, bought a couple of cheap paperback novels, and filled my pantry as if I were settling in for a long winter, despite the heat of late July.

One day, out of sheer boredom, I drove to Sturgis just to see what all the fuss was about. The rally was only a week away, and the town already hummed with anticipation. Bikes were rumbling through the streets, riders staking out their favorite spots, and souvenir shops buzzing as they braced for the chaos ahead. Even back in International Falls, we'd heard the stories about rally week, the kind that made Vegas blush. Standing there, watching Sturgis rev up for what was coming, I couldn't help but wonder what the place would feel like once it tipped fully into madness.

Amber had been my only visitor. Her text surprised me, coming just a few days after the *incident*, which I'd started calling it in my head. I couldn't bring myself to use the word *altercation* as the legal forms did. That word felt too sterile.

She'd brought baby Wyatt with her, his tiny fingers wrapped in a blue blanket. She let me hold him, and I'd forgotten how light a baby could be. The smell of baby powder and milk clung to him, and something inside me ached. My maternal clock, silenced over the last two years, began to tick again. If Mitch had lived, would I have been a mother by now? Would our baby have had his eyes? His laugh?

Amber must have caught whatever flashed across my face, because she gently shifted the conversation. She told me that more nurses had begun whispering about Dr. Adams. Not formal complaints, not accusations, just confusing stories about women who'd been there one day and gone the next. No one ever explained why. At the time, Amber had chalked it up to burnout, better job offers, or personal issues. But now, after hearing what Ford had done to me, she couldn't help wondering if there had been a pattern all along. If those disappearances hadn't been coincidences at all.

Her words left an unsettling hollow space inside me, a quiet echo where all my anger had been. And now, with confirmation that I could return to work the next morning, I told myself I was ready. Ready to walk back in. Ready to settle into my role again. Ready to start fresh, whatever *fresh* looked like now.

My life, I thought. *Just me. Alone.* And I was okay with that. At least that's what I kept telling myself.

The next morning came early.

I arrived at the hospital just after six thirty. When I checked in with Mr. Jackson, he greeted me with a slight nod. I was surprised to see him there, actually. But it was a small hospital, and I supposed someone had to be there to welcome me back.

"Welcome back, Nurse Cassidy," he said, sliding my ID badge across the desk.

"Thank you," I said.

He hesitated, then added, "You should know that Mr. Adams has been relieved of his post as hospitalist. Dr. Nelson will be taking over his duties for now."

There it was again: the pointed use of *"Mr."* instead of *"Dr."* I gave a small nod. "That's probably for the best."

The rest of the day passed in a haze of patient charts, rounds, and catching up on everything I'd missed. It felt strange to be back, but also grounding. The hospital's rhythm was familiar. Predictable. And after two weeks of isolation while on administrative leave, predictable felt good.

By the end of my shift, exhaustion had settled deep into my bones. I was ready to head home, shower, and eat something that didn't come out of a vending machine. But when I reached the parking lot, I stopped short. Parked beside my Cadillac SUV was a black BMW sedan. Sleek. Polished. Familiar. Dane.

He stepped out of the car, looking just as devastatingly composed as ever. Dark jeans, black button-down, sleeves rolled to his forearms.

A light wind tousled his hair. He held up a hand as I opened my mouth to speak.

"Brooke," he began, his voice calm. "I know you have a lot of questions. I understand why you wouldn't want to speak with me. But I came here to apologize for what happened, and for what I didn't tell you. I want the chance to explain everything."

For a moment, I couldn't move. Couldn't breathe. My heart was hammering, but not just from anger. Because the truth was, I'd missed him.

I wanted to be mad. I wanted to tell him to leave, to let me be. But there was that same tug in my chest, the one I'd felt the first time he'd looked at me across the Silver Spur dining room.

Maybe it was the loneliness talking. Or it was something deeper. With the end of my contract drawing closer with every week, what did I have to lose? Ford was gone. I was safe. At least, I believed I was.

I nodded once, taking a slow breath. "Fine," I said. "I'll listen. But we'll do it on my terms, somewhere neutral. Not at your casino, not at the restaurant. And not tonight. I need time, Dane."

He looked down at the asphalt, his jaw tightening, and for a second, I thought I saw something raw in his expression. Regret, maybe. Or sorrow.

"Wherever you want, Brooke," he said quietly. "Just give me the chance to tell you why I didn't tell you about Ford."

I nodded again and took a step back toward my car. "I'll text you after my shift tomorrow. We'll figure something out then."

He didn't argue. Didn't push. Just stood there, hands in his pockets, watching me.

As I drove away, I checked my rearview mirror. He was still there, standing in the same spot, the summer breeze tugging at his shirt, the shadows of the parking lot stretching long around him.

And for the first time in the last two weeks, I wasn't sure whether driving away was the right thing to do.

Chapter 15

Even though I had told Dane I would text him the next day, I'd let another few days pass before finally deciding it was time to talk. I'd done a lot of reflecting, and I still believed everyone deserved a chance to explain themselves. Besides, I missed him, truly missed him. Not just the sex, though I'd be lying if I said I hadn't caught myself replaying the feel of his hands, his mouth, the way he looked at me like I was the only woman in the room, or on the back steps of his porch. But it went deeper than that. It wasn't about missing someone to touch me; it was about missing *him*. His quiet humor. The way his voice softened when he said my name. The calm I felt just being near him.

So, I texted him. Told him I wanted a *proper* date. Not at The Silver Spur. Not in his world, where he always seemed to hold the upper hand. I wanted neutral ground, somewhere he couldn't hide behind charm or control. I told him to take me to dinner at another casino in town, one of his competitors. Let him play by someone else's rules for once.

By Saturday night, I was ready. Dane pulled up at exactly seven, ever punctual, ever composed. I stepped out of my house wearing a short black strapless cocktail dress that hugged my curves and ended just high enough to make him swallow hard when I approached. My hair was down, soft waves brushing my shoulders, and I'd swiped on red lipstick that matched my heels and the paint on my toes and fingernails. For the first time in weeks, I felt like me again.

He smiled when he saw me, that slow, deliberate smile that always made my pulse trip. "You look… incredible," he said, opening the passenger door.

I slid in and smoothed my dress over my thighs. "Remember," I said, teasingly. "Best behavior tonight."

His grin widened. "I'll do my best, Ms. Cassidy. Though I make no promises if you keep looking like that."

We drove to the Gold Mine Casino, one of Deadwood's newer establishments. It was a little glitzier, a little less steeped in the town's old charm. Inside, the air smelled faintly of perfume and whiskey. The restaurant was upscale but cozy, tucked away from the noise of the gaming floor. Over flickering candlelight and the soft noise of conversation, I looked at Dane and decided it was time to lay everything out.

"Tell me," I said, setting my napkin down. "All of it. No half-truths, no skimming past the ugly parts. I want to know why you never told me Ford was your brother."

Dane leaned back, shoulders tightening as though bracing himself. His gaze drifted toward the window before returning to me. "When my mother was dying," he began, voice low, "she made me promise I'd look after him. Give him a place to live. A job. Some kind of foundation. She always believed he could turn things around if someone kept him on task."

He rubbed a hand along his jaw. "I thought she meant the usual trouble, like late nights, bad decisions, stupid fights. But over these last two weeks of the investigations... I've learned a lot more than she ever told me. I've had people digging. Looking through old hospital records, settlements, and HR reports that never saw daylight. And yes," he exhaled, slow and heavy, "I threw some money around to get answers."

My stomach tightened. "What did you find?"

Dane hesitated only a moment. "My mom paid off women. Multiple women." His expression twisted, disgusted, not at them, but at the truth. "Accusations of sexual harassment, going back years. She kept it all quiet. Checks were filed under 'miscellaneous hospital donations.' Lawyers handled the rest. No one ever used the word 'assault,' not officially. But Brooke..." His eyes met mine. "After what happened to you, I don't believe for a second that harassment was the worst of it."

A chill worked its way down my spine. "Your mother actually paid women to keep silent?"

He nodded, shame pulling at the edges of his expression. "She thought she was protecting him and protecting our family. I don't think she ever understood what she was covering. Or maybe she did, and she just couldn't face it."

I sat back, stunned. "That's horrifying. Women came forward about a powerful doctor and were paid to disappear. And she let that continue?"

His jaw tightened. "Ford never stopped when he wanted something. Never. And I think when he realized you and I were... involved, he pushed even further. He always had a competitive streak, but this—" He shook his head. "This was him crossing a line he never should have been anywhere near."

I swallowed hard, anger rising in my chest, not at Dane, but at the years of women who had tried to speak and been told their voices didn't matter.

Dane reached for my hand, more cautious than I'd ever seen him. "I've spent the last two weeks working with my attorneys and some people in law enforcement. Ford is gone. He agreed to leave Deadwood permanently."

"Where?" I asked.

"Montana. A ranch." He paused. "And before you worry, he won't be without supervision. Let's just say the men checking in on him are the type of people you don't want to irritate. His brow lifted slightly. "Nothing illegal. Just... persuasive."

I blew out a breath, interpreting exactly what he meant. These men were likely of the break-your-kneecap-to-get-the-point-across type. And somehow, I was fine with that. Ford wouldn't be hurting anyone else anytime soon.

"And you think that fixes this?" I finally asked, voice quieter than I intended.

"No." Dane shook his head. "It won't undo what happened. But it keeps him away from you. And away from anyone else he might hurt."

The sincerity on his face, the raw apology behind his eyes, was something I hadn't expected to see. Not from a man so controlled, so careful.

"I'm asking for your forgiveness," he continued. "For not telling you sooner. For not protecting you sooner. For not taking the time to realize what he really was."

I watched him for a long moment, letting silence settle between us.

"I don't know if I can forgive all of it," I said finally. "But I can forgive you for trying."

Relief flickered across his features, softening the tension in his shoulders.

"But listen to me, Dane," I added, leaning in. "If you ever hide something like this again, something that matters, I won't be this understanding next time."

He nodded, solemn enough to make it feel like an oath. "Understood."

For a moment, neither of us spoke. Then another thought pulled at me. "What happens now," I asked quietly, "with the money? The funds your casino has been sending to the hospital every year?"

His expression shifted, the tension returning, but different this time. Calculated. Resolved. "I've already stopped all transfers," he said. "Every cent. An investigation is underway to see who at the hospital knew... who helped keep things quiet." His voice darkened. "When it all comes to light, those people won't be working in Deadwood again. Not in healthcare. Not anywhere close to women who depend on them."

My stomach twisted with a mix of anger and something like relief. "Good." Then, after a beat, "But maybe those funds shouldn't disappear."

His eyes narrowed slightly, curious.

"What if," I said, choosing my words carefully, "instead of sending the money back into the same account, we redirect it somewhere that actually helps women? Programs for survivors of sexual assault or domestic violence. Places that don't rely on silence."

Dane watched me, really watched me, and something shifted behind his eyes. It was something like pride. "That's a damn good idea," he said. Then he paused, shook his head once. "But I've got a better one."

I lifted a brow. "Better than supporting organizations that already do the work?"

A slow smile spread across his face, edged with possibility. "We start something here," he said. "In South Dakota. A resource center. Counseling, legal help, emergency housing... whatever women in crisis need." His jaw tightened. "Somewhere real. Somewhere safe. A place that doesn't hide predators. One that stops them."

My chest warmed at the conviction in his voice. "You'd fund all of that?"

"I'd fund it with my last dollar," he said simply. "But I'd want you to help shape it. You'd understand what victims actually need far better than I ever could."

For a moment, I just let his words settle. Then another thought surfaced, practical, but still necessary. "And what about the hospital?" I asked. "Some of that money did help. The problem wasn't the hospital. It was the people who allowed Ford to keep working there. And they're being dealt with. But the ER" I hesitated, recalling Amber's wish list: updated monitors, new trauma carts, and improved family rooms for loved ones waiting through emergencies. "There's a lot that could use support."

He nodded slowly. "I'll ask for a full review, department by department. Once we know what's needed, I'll allocate funds where they do the most good. I'm not pulling support from the community, Brooke. I'm pulling support from the people who abused it."

The distinction landed with surprising clarity. "Good," I murmured. "Then maybe we can do both. Help the hospital do better... and help women who need it."

Dane's fingers brushed mine, warm and certain. "We will," he said. "All of it."

The idea hung between us. It was larger than both of us, but suddenly I felt I had a new purpose in life. Something to help me continue moving forward after all I lost in Minnesota. "You have the resources to do that?" I asked.

He leaned in, threading his fingers through mine. "I have the resources to do just about anything, Brooke. But this... this I would want to do with you."

My breath caught, because it wasn't a romantic declaration, not exactly. It was something more profound. A commitment. A path forward.

And for the first time in weeks, the tension in my chest eased, just a little. For the first time since everything happened, I felt like we were finally standing on something real. Messy, complicated, but real.

Dinner carried on, lighter now, both of us testing the edges of peace. When we finished, I pushed back from the table and smiled. "Show me the tables."

He blinked. "The poker tables?"

"Yes," I said. "You told me all about them earlier. Let's see if your rival runs a tighter ship than you do."

He laughed, and soon we were weaving through the casino floor, the sound of chips and laughter surrounding us. Dane pointed out the blackjack and roulette tables, explaining odds and strategies, his voice smooth. But just as we reached the high-limit poker room, his phone buzzed. He frowned when he saw the caller ID.

"I need to take this," he muttered, stepping aside. His tone shifted immediately. It was low, sharp, authoritative. "Handle it quietly," I heard him say. "I'm on my way."

He hung up and looked at me, jaw tight. "I'm sorry. There's been an altercation at The Silver Spur. A bachelor party got out of hand. I need to go. Please come with me?"

Something in his eyes told me this wasn't a request. And truth be told, I didn't want the night to end. I nodded.

Back at The Silver Spur, Dane led me through a side corridor I hadn't noticed before and into a private suite off the private dining room we had dined in a few weeks earlier. "We use this for special events," he said.

The room was dimly lit, elegant but intimate. A long mahogany table sat in the center, surrounded by plush chairs. A polished bar lined one wall, and a smaller poker table gleamed in the corner beneath a hanging chandelier.

"Will you wait for me here?" he asked softly.

I nodded, and he disappeared through the door.

Desmond appeared a few minutes later with a chilled glass of Chardonnay and a reassuring smile. "Mr. Walker asked me to bring you this to keep you company."

"Thank you," I said, settling into one of the chairs around the large table. I watched as Desmond left the room.

By the time Dane returned half an hour later, the wine was gone, my nerves beginning to soothe. His shirt was unbuttoned at the collar, his hair slightly mussed.

"The men have been escorted out," he said, exhaling. "Bachelor party gone sideways. Nothing serious."

I stood up from the chair at the end of the table and leaned my weight against it. I held out my empty wine glass. "It's empty," I said.

Dane walked toward me and removed the glass from my hand. He walked over to the bar and set it down, his back to me. "I know you told me to behave. But how can you expect me to when you wear a dress like that? You're a beautiful woman, Brooke."

I looked down at my dress, then held up my hands and admired the red nail polish. As a nurse, it wasn't an indulgence I often enjoyed. "You're not so bad-looking yourself, Dane," I said, watching him as he turned to me. I wondered where the night would go. And thankfully, he didn't leave me guessing.

He crossed the room and took me in his arms. His mouth met mine as he placed one hand behind my neck and wrapped his other arm around my back, pulling me to him. I could feel his hardness under the thin fabric of my dress. Before I knew what he was doing, he had shoved the chair from the end of the table out of his way, and he was lifting me up and onto the table.

He pushed me back so that I was lying on the table, and I moaned as he raked his hands down my body. "Dane," I uttered, my breath hitching as he reached up under my dress and swore as he discovered I was not wearing any panties. I had removed them while I waited for him to deal with the bachelor party situation.

"Brooke, what are you doing to me? I thought you told me to be on my best behavior," he growled as he pushed my dress up around my hips, leaving me bare and exposed. "You make me so hungry," he said as he bent forward and laid his mouth on me. His tongue was teasing at first, licking me up and down both sides. But then, he took my clit in his mouth and sucked, hard. I bucked at the feeling of the pain and pleasure.

"Not wearing any panties," he mouthed into my pussy. "That's a very naughty girl, and you should be punished."

I grabbed his hair with my hands and pulled his face closer to where I needed. He rewarded me by plunging his tongue in between my folds, in and out, making me so wet that I was dripping. I opened my eyes and looked up at the ceiling, noticing the security cameras posted strategically throughout the room. I almost stopped him, but then his mouth sucked in my clit again, and he replaced his tongue with one, two, and then three of his fingers. Fucking me with his hand. Taking me for all that I am.

"Dane, I want you to fuck me," I said, finally finding the words to answer the question he had been asking me all those weeks ago.

But Dane had other plans for me. "I will fuck you, Brooke, but first I will defile you, and you will enjoy every moment of it," he growled again into my center. With the fingers of his right hand still inside me, he reached around with his left hand and massaged that gentle opening of my asshole, and I groaned in pleasure.

I'd always been curious about anal exploration, but it had just never gone anywhere with Mitch. Now, I felt guilty, not because of what

I was doing with Dane, but of thinking of Mitch during this intense sexual encounter.

Satisfied that I was opening up to him, Dane plunged the index finger of his left hand inside, and that was all I needed to lose myself. I climaxed hard. I was still coming down when Dane removed his fingers and pulled my body closer to him, wrapping me around him. He picked me up and carried me over to the poker table, depositing my bare ass on the edge of the table.

I started to speak, but he silenced me by shoving those three fingers from his right hand into my mouth, beckoning me to suck away my own juices. As I did, he used his free hand to lower the zipper on the back of my dress. He pushed me back, and I wiggled as he pulled the dress down, my breasts now loose. He helped me sit up again and then shoved me backward. "Scoot to the middle of the table, Brooke," he said.

I looked at him questioningly, not sure what he wanted. "Let's play some poker of our own."

I scooted back and watched as he hoisted himself up onto the table, crawling toward me and my naked body. "You have too many clothes on," I protested, and he looked down, almost as if actually realizing that he wasn't yet naked.

"We can take care of that later. I'm not done tasting you yet," he said. "Get on all fours," he whispered as he flipped himself over onto his back. I turned, and as though he were on a mechanic's creeper, he moved himself under me, his face now under my pussy. "Sit."

"I—" I wasn't sure about that. It wasn't something I had ever done before, but the idea of sitting on Dane's face was entirely intriguing. "I don't know what to do," I breathed, my arousal growing as I looked down and underneath me to see his head raise. I felt his tongue lashing my clitoris. It felt divine.

"Lower yourself and move to give yourself what you want," he said. I did what he asked. As I lowered myself onto his face, I found that I could quickly control my pleasure, shifting myself to just what I needed. Within moments, I came again and felt myself leaking out over his chin.

Dane reached down and removed his pants, quickly scooting up and taking my mouth with his. This too was new to me. Mitch and I had rarely engaged in any type of oral pleasure, and when we did, we had always cleaned ourselves up before engaging in any further activity. I realized now just how much more there was to intimacy.

"Lower yourself onto me, Brooke," he said, but I hesitated. I could see how erect his cock was. Though I knew I had taken him before, Dane had been on top the last time. This time, I would need to take all of him, and I wondered if he would fit.

As if sensing my concern, Dane whispered, "You can take me, baby, just open yourself up." And I did. Grateful for my deceivingly strong legs, despite their skinniness, I rocked back and forth and eased myself down onto him. I placed my hands on my breasts, squeezing my nipples with my hands while he watched. He filled me wholly and completely. He grasped my hips and bucked into me. I felt my eyes roll into the back of my head as I enjoyed the sensation. A small smile pulled up my lips as I realized we were literally fucking on a poker table in the private room of Dane's casino.

Dane started to growl, and though I didn't think it was possible, I felt his erection grow inside of me. And just moments later, I felt the heat of his orgasm, vigorous and intense. It was just what I needed for my own climax to find me. I rocked and gyrated my hips, indulging in the feel.

As I came, I looked down at him and saw him staring at me in wonder. "Brooke, I think I'm in love with you," he said. It was sweet and sincere, but as though he needed to make a true impact, he bucked once more, and I felt my insides literally explode around him once again.

If I could say anything about my sex life with Dane, it would be that it left nothing to mystery. That night in the private gaming room of his casino, on the long mahogany table and yes, on the poker table, I realized something I had been trying not to admit to myself:

I was absolutely in love with Dane Walker. Emotionally. Physically. Wholly.

And though the sex was incredible, that wasn't the whole story. I kept replaying the moments after my *fourth* orgasm of the night, when he had helped me down from the poker table, careful with my body, holding me as though I were something precious. He'd wrapped his suit jacket around my naked skin, the fabric warm from his own heat. I watched him pull on his underwear and pants with quick, practiced movements, then he lifted me into his arms and carried me to the oversized couch tucked into the corner of the room.

We curled there together, tangled and breathless. We talked. Kissed. Traced each other's skin like we were trying to memorize the shape of something we weren't ready to lose. And yes, we may have made love once or twice more. The man was incorrigible.

But what struck me wasn't only the demanding, scorching sex on the tables. It was how the night shifted afterward into something softer, quieter, threaded with a kind of tenderness I hadn't expected. A tenderness that made me realize I wasn't just falling for Dane... I was finding my footing again and finding purpose. Somehow, in the chaos of being hurt and then choosing to rise anyway, I'd uncovered a strength I didn't know I had, one I could use to help others who'd been through their own terrifying moments. And beneath all of that, reliable and undeniable, was something that felt suspiciously, terrifyingly like love.

Chapter 16

After that night at The Gold Mine and then at the Silver Spur, I'd done a lot of thinking. More, I think, than I had allowed myself to do since Mitch died. When I first arrived in Deadwood, I'd seen the next twelve weeks as a pause button for my life. A place to hide, to gather myself, and maybe, if I was lucky, to start feeling like a whole person again.

I'd believed grief had a set shape. That healing had to look a certain way, full of quiet reflection, long walks, sleeping alone, staying busy. I'd told myself that time and distance would eventually mend a broken heart if I just followed the "right" pattern.

But, as it turns out, grief isn't tidy. It isn't predictable. And it isn't something you must shoulder in isolation. It changes alongside you. It softens corners you never planned to revisit. And sometimes, if you're open to it, compassion slips in when you least expect it, wrapped in the arms of a man you weren't looking for.

In the weeks that followed, Dane and I spent long stretches together, talking through our pasts and slowly revealing the pieces we had tucked away. He'd been gentle with my memories of Mitch, never once making me feel wrong for still loving someone who was no longer here. He told me more than once that he didn't expect me to be "finished" with my grief. "How could you be?" he had said one night as we lay tangled in his bed. "He was your first love. You don't lose someone like that and just close the door behind you."

And because he was honest, I felt safe enough to ask about his first love. He told me her name. Margie. The girl who had gotten away when her family moved after high school. They'd kept in touch for a while, but life has a habit of shifting people in different directions. Eventually, they both moved on.

We also discussed other items. More intimate things. Our sex lives, the choices we'd made, the people we'd been with. Dane didn't shy away. When I asked bluntly about the rumors of him being a womanizer, he didn't deny them. He told me he'd had a full dating life for years, but about two years ago, he said, something shifted. It hadn't been one moment, but a gradual realization that casual connections weren't fulfilling him anymore. He didn't want nights that ended as quickly as they began. He wanted something that stayed. Something that mattered.

Ironically, that shift happened around the time Mitch died. I wasn't sure what to do with that coincidence, but it sat with me. And then came the question I had been avoiding: What was *I* going to do once Amber returned from maternity leave?

That answer became a bit easier when Paul Jackson informed me that Amber had resigned. She wanted to stay home with her baby.

She'd recommended that the hospital offer me her position. I'd been floored. I'd also been terrified.

I spent two full days mulling over the offer in my mind. Accepting it meant real, permanent change. It meant choosing Deadwood not just as a temporary escape, but as a place to plant myself. It also meant something else… something I hadn't been able to shake since my dinner with Dane.

If I stayed, building the organization we discussed would be easier. More possible. South Dakota wasn't just where I'd ended up; it was turning into the place where I could actually *do* something.

Still, I didn't want Dane to think I was choosing any of this *because* of him. What we had was still new. Intense, yes, but still settling into shape. I'd expected him to be cautious, maybe even hesitant.

Instead, when I told him, he lit up like someone had handed him an unexpected gift.

"I'd love for you to stay," he told me, voice low and grounded. "Not for me. For *you.* You're brilliant at what you do. They'd be lucky to have you. But we, together, could do so much."

His reaction spilled warmth through me that I wasn't prepared for.

I spent time on the phone with my mom, my oldest brother's wife, and even Mitch's mother. I told them about the offer, about the town, and, without getting into details, about Dane and my plans to help women who needed it. To my surprise, every one of them encouraged me. They told me I deserved happiness and a fresh start. That Mitch would have wanted me to keep living, not stay stuck out of loyalty to a future we never got to have. And that Mitch would have been proud of me.

So the choice became clear.

Just two weeks before the end of my contract, I walked into Paul Jackson's office and asked if the offer still stood. When he said yes, I accepted without hesitation. Later that afternoon, after signing the contract, I left the office as the new lead charge nurse for the emergency department.

It felt surreal. Thrilling. A little terrifying. But right.

That left only one major question: Where would I live?

Commuting from Rapid City wasn't practical. Forty-five minutes each way after twelve-hour shifts would wear on anyone, especially in winter. The small house I'd been renting in Deadwood was no longer an option; the owner had already booked another tenant to move in as soon as I moved out.

So Dane and I made a plan.

When I worked, I'd stay in the penthouse apartment at the casino. On my off days, I'd be wherever Dane happened to be. That means sometimes Deadwood and sometimes Rapid City. He spent more time at the Rapid City home in the off-season, when the casino slowed down.

It wasn't a perfect arrangement, but it felt manageable. And natural. And, if I were being honest, comforting.

Still, there was one more decision to make. The house Mitch and I had shared in International Falls. The place is full of memories. The place I had clung to, unsure if letting it go meant letting go of him.

But standing in my small rental kitchen one afternoon, phone pressed to my ear as I spoke with my realtor in Minnesota, I realized that sometimes moving forward requires letting go of the weight that holds you in place.

I loved Mitch. I would always love Mitch. But selling the house didn't erase him. It didn't erase who we had been. It simply made space for who I was becoming. And I was becoming someone new.

Someone who could build a life in a historic town in the Black Hills. Someone who could fall deeply, feverishly in love with a man like Dane Walker. Someone who could stand on her own two feet, no matter whose arms she fell asleep in.

Deadwood had changed me, slowly, quietly, in ways I hadn't expected. It had surprised me and pushed me beyond the version of myself I'd arrived with. Within a matter of weeks, I had signed the paperwork for my new position, arranged to sell my house, and packed up the last of my belongings in International Falls. Through all of it, one thought stayed with me: I wasn't losing myself. I was finding a new version of my life.

A life built in a town where grit and beauty coexist. A life with a man who challenged me, comforted me, turned me on, and frustrated me, sometimes in the same breath—a life shaped not by fear of the past, but by hope for what came next.

And in this life, my life, the house always wins.

Epilogue

It's astonishing how much a life can change in the span of a year, or in my case, in the span of three. Around this time three years ago, I had been lying on a blanket in California, sun-drunk and tipsy, feeding olives to my fiancé, Mitch Raines. I remember laughing, teasing him, thinking about our future with the kind of naïve certainty that comes with young love.

Now, Mitch is gone, and though the ache hasn't disappeared entirely, it no longer crushes me the way it once did. The sharp edges have softened, and the memories feel more like warmth than wounds. I still miss him, and I always will. But I've learned that grief doesn't erase the ability to love again.

Today, I have a job that truly fulfills me. And I have a man who, after everything we've faced and everything we've uncovered, I can say, without hesitation, is the love of my life.

The investigation at the hospital wrapped up several months ago. Paul Jackson proved instrumental in bringing the truth to the surface.

The very administrator he had replaced was the one siphoning funds and orchestrating payoffs that had protected men like Ford for far too long. That chapter is closed now. And Paul didn't just stop there. He approached Dane and me, offering to be a resource for the organization we're building, particularly for women who need confidential medical care and trauma support. Knowing we have an ally inside the healthcare system gives me hope for what we can build.

Through all of this, Dane and I have grown in ways I never anticipated. I've learned he's far more tender than the world ever sees, and he's learned how to let me in piece by piece, even the darker corners of himself he once kept locked away. His rough edges are still there, of course. I wouldn't want them gone, but they've softened, shaped by honesty and a willingness to share the emotional weight he used to shoulder alone.

Because we're building something designed to help women reclaim their power after losing it, we've worked hard to ensure our own relationship honors boundaries as well. One night, after a long conversation about the stories we'd heard, we came up with a safe word. "Poker table." Fitting, considering how our chemistry tends to flare in places we shouldn't touch each other... but we haven't needed to use it. Not yet, anyway.

That's not to say our sex life has lost its fire, far from it. It's still hot and frantic and full of all the delicious heat that drew us together in the first place. But now there's something layered beneath it, too. Something deeper. Something real. And, well... we've had some memorable adventures.

One of my favorites was our return to Cathedral Spires. We didn't exactly recreate our first visit. Not exactly. This time, it was more of a role reversal. My idea, though I'm fairly sure Dane had gone into the day assuming he'd be the one in charge.

He was wrong.

I'd surprised him when I pushed him against the rock wall, dropped to my knees, and unbuttoned his shorts. They hit the ground in a soft thud, and before he could even process what was happening, I had his massive cock in my mouth. I almost lost my nerve when I heard hikers coming up the trail, but the thrill of it, the wickedness of doing something so bold in the wild, kept me going. Dane didn't stop me. I think he was too startled, too undone, too overtaken by the shock of me taking control.

His fingers tightened in my hair as he moaned, "Fuck, Brooke," over and over again, his voice echoing faintly off the stone. Whether those hikers kept going because they didn't know the hideaway existed, or because they heard the sounds we were making and decided to give us space, or because they were voyeuristic little deviants who stood there silently watching, I didn't know. And honestly? I didn't care. In that moment, it was about giving Dane pleasure. And the way he exploded in my mouth told me exactly how much he enjoyed it.

He came hard, and to his shock, and, let's be honest, my own, I swallowed every drop. I'd never imagined I would do something like that, but with Dane, so much of what I thought I knew about myself had shifted.

He'd been so wrecked afterward that I was certain he'd take me against the rocks again, but even I had limits when it came to public indecency. So I helped him pull up his shorts, and we made a wobbly, laughing retreat to my SUV parked at the far end of the lot.

And because I'd planned that day down to the last detail, I'd insisted he get in the back seat. My SUV had far more room than his sedan. He listened, that dazed, hungry look still in his eyes, and climbed in. I had worn a sporty little skirt, and when I crawled in after him and hiked it up, revealing I had skipped the panties entirely, he went utterly still.

Then I lowered myself onto his cock and rode him in the back seat of that SUV, both of us trying (and failing) to stay quiet. I ground myself forward and back, giving myself the pressure I needed to bring me to orgasm. And he pushed up into me, helping me to take every inch. He came undone. I came undone. Twice. Thank you very much.

But Dane apparently had his own surprise planned that day.

Later, when we drove the wildlife loop again and came up on the donkeys, he told me to pull over. We got out, apples and carrots in hand, and the donkeys trotted up to us with their usual bold charm. I was laughing as one nudged my arm, when I turned around and found that Dane was no longer beside me.

He was on one knee. A baby-blue box was open in one hand, an enormous diamond glittering in the sunlight. In the other hand, he held a bottle of hand sanitizer. I burst out laughing because nothing says romance quite like donkey slobber and Purell.

He waited patiently while I cleaned my hands and tucked the sanitizer into my cross-body bag. Then he proposed, right there on the roadside, with donkeys watching and strangers gathering around us with phones out. It was absurd, perfect, and entirely unforgettable.

And of course, I said yes.

At this stage of life, with my mid-thirties staring me in the face, I wasn't interested in a long engagement or months of planning. I'd done that once already. I wanted something intimate, simple, and honest. Thankfully, Dane wanted the same.

So yesterday, in the backyard of his Rapid City home, with the Black Hills rising strong behind us, surrounded by my family, several friends, and even Mitch's parents, we got married.

Today is the morning after. I'm in our bed, in our house, in this modest but beautiful home that now belongs to both of us.

Well, I'm technically lying in bed. My legs are spread wide and draped over Dane's shoulders as he pleasures me with his mouth. And, well, let's just say it's a very good morning. A very, very good morning. And as I arch beneath him, breathless and alive, I can't help thinking that life, for all its twists and heartbreaks and unexpected turns, brought me exactly where I was meant to be.

Here. With him. In this wild, historic little corner of the world, where everything changed for me.

A Final Note

Before you close this book, I want to pause for something important. *The House Always Wins* is meant to be a fun, flirty, and an undeniably sexy story about desire, second chances, and finding your footing again. But it also touches on a moment where a sexual advance is not wanted, not invited, and not okay. That distinction matters, and it's one I don't take lightly.

Sexual harassment and sexual assault are crimes. They violate trust, safety, and autonomy. According to RAINN (Rape, Abuse & Incest National Network), nearly every minute someone in the United States is sexually assaulted. Many never come forward. Many carry the weight of what happened in silence, unsure of what to say, who to trust, or whether they'll be believed.

If parts of this story felt uncomfortable, heavy, or close to home, please know this: you are not alone. What happened to you is not your fault. Support is available and provided without judgment.

If you believe you have experienced sexual harassment or sexual assault, you can contact the National Sexual Assault Hotline at 1-800-656-HOPE (4673). You'll be connected with a trained advocate who can listen, offer support, and help you understand your options, whether or not you choose to take action.

This story is fiction. The reality it touches on in the scene between Ford and Brooke is not. If you or someone you love needs help, please reach out. You deserve safety, care, and to be heard.

Acknowledgments

When the opportunity to participate in the *Wild Deadwood Reads 2026 Anthology* landed in my inbox, I didn't hesitate. I didn't actually raise my hand in the air, but I *did* fill out the form and say, "Yes, absolutely, sign me up." Because the chance to write a story set against the backdrop of the Black Hills? That was impossible to resist.

I've been lucky enough to spend time in the Black Hills and in Deadwood over the years, and it's one of those places that lingers with you long after you leave. I have fond memories of traveling there with my dad and sister for a snowmobiling trip in the dead of winter (pun very much intended), and later returning with my kids when they were young. There's something about the landscape, rugged, dramatic, and just a little wild, that felt like the perfect setting for a story that wasn't going to play it safe.

And then there was the added bonus: the flexibility to release this story as a standalone novella, with extra scenes and bonus content beyond the anthology. That opened the door to a much bigger question: what kind of story did I want to tell?

So I asked my readers. And the answer came back loud and clear: spice.

I'll be honest. Writing a spicy story was relatively new territory for me. Exciting, intimidating, and slightly nerve-wracking all at once. Would I pull it off? Would readers connect with it? Would it feel like me on the page? The only way to find out was to do the thing. And along the way, I learned a lot, not just about writing heat, but about my own voice, my instincts, and where I still want to grow.

So yes, my first thank-you goes to this novella itself. It pushed me. It surprised me. And it made me a stronger writer on the other side.

Of course, I didn't get here alone.

Huge thanks to Ginger Ring and Linda Rae Sande, the hosts of Wild Deadwood Reads, for creating what is already one of the most thoughtfully organized and welcoming book events I've ever been part of. Even before setting foot in Deadwood for the festival, it's been clear how much care and passion go into this event.

To my editor, Kiersten Hall of Fox Pointe Publishing, thank you for your sharp eye, thoughtful feedback, and for helping shape this story into something tighter, stronger, and more emotionally grounded.

And to Scotty Town, my cover and interior designer. Once again, you nailed it. I've heard nothing but wonderful feedback on the covers you've created for my books, and this one is no exception.

To my husband, Scott. Thank you for supporting this dream, even when it's messy, time-consuming, or just plain exhausting. Having your ongoing encouragement means more than you know.

To my kids, my friends, and especially the Minnesota Bookstagram community, your enthusiasm, your messages, and your constant cheering from the sidelines keep me going on the days when the words come a little slower.

And finally, to my readers: thank you. For showing up. For trusting me with your time. For growing alongside me as I try new things and tell new kinds of stories. Without you, none of this would matter.

Here's to what comes next.

www.ingramcontent.com/pod-product-compliance
Lightning Source LLC
LaVergne TN
LVHW050410080526
838231LV00045B/1107

9798993850474